PET ACADEMY

SIDRA KHAN

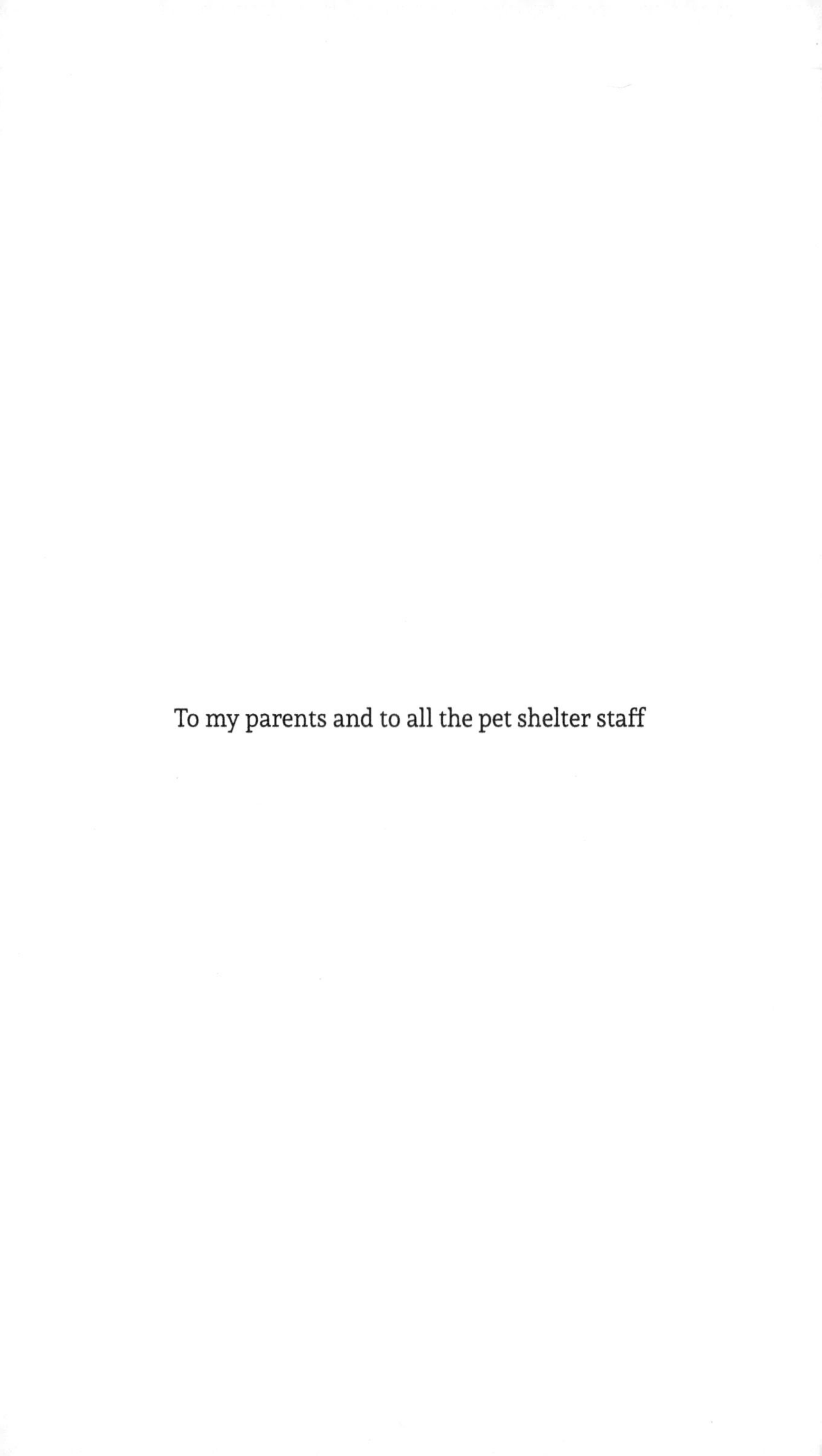

To my parents and to all the pet shelter staff

Contents

Contents

1

The Letter

Pet academy was like a boarding school, except the school focused on teaching children more about animal care, it was a great school for anyone who wanted to be a vet, pet sitter or anything related to animals, but the thing was that it was very difficult to get into it.

That's why Aurora Stargaze was very shocked when she got the letter, confirming her admission into the wonderful academy. Really, because this Pet academy was for people who had some special connection with animals.

"Aurora! Go check the mail box, I saw a post man today" Her mother called out

Aurora tutted and put away her book of Pet care, *it's probably some silly spam, no one writes these days.* Aurora had applied for admission in pet academy, but she just forgot about it because she thought that she wouldn't be admitted.

But when she opened the mail box, her annoyance was ripped apart, because in front of the letter, in glossy writing was written

Pet academy

She tore open the letter and read the words

Dear Aurora Stargaze,

We are happy to announce that you officially are one of our students. The bus to our academy will come at you address in 10 A.M. in 11 March. Every weekend you can visit your parents if they are not too far away.

You will have to bring the following things:

1. A pet- A cat, horse, dog or rabbit one pet per person

2. Your essential things-clothes and things like that

3. The books mentioned in the below list- yes, they are important

There will be summer holidays and Christmas breaks along the two years you will be spending in our school.

You don't have to bring your pet essentials because our academy has them all, but if your pet has a favourite toy or blanket you may bring it along.

If you are bringing a horse, please tell us so we will send a horse transportation vehicle along.

The rest of the rules and regulations will be explained once you reach the school doors.

Regards,

School principal Victoria Avanza

Aurora turned over and saw some other pages, receipts and other boring things particularly for her parents, she also saw the book list, one of them was the book she was reading just right now. She didn't have a pet, not yet. but her parents had said they would buy her a pet soon, a cat.

"Aurora! What's taking you so long!" her mom called

Aurora ran into the house and shouted

"Mom! Mom! I have been selected to the school"

"What??" Her mom replied, her voice thick with disbelief

Aurora nodded and showed her the crumpled letter.

2

2 days later

Aurora Stargaze's life wasn't normal, she was her parent's only child, her dad went out to work and mom often had to go out too... In school she also had problems because she was different.

She was quiet and nerdy then the other kids, she didn't go to parties when invited, she was shy in such gatherings and avoided them. Aurora had no friends, so school became her fear. Also, she loved animals and that's why everyone often found her strange.

Strange and quiet were the only words she often heard for herself. But then she soon found out about this pet academy, she knew that if she got admitted, she wouldn't only find more about taking care animals, but she had a chance to meet like-minded people and have friends.

Tomorrow would be the day she would be sitting on the bus to her dream school.

They had already brought the books yesterday, they had also asked for a math, history and English books because they would be teaching those things too.

Today they would be going to the shelter to buy a cat.

"Aurora dear, come in! We will be late," Her mom called out from the car

Aurora ran and sat inside, her heart beating at the prospect of actually getting a cat.

"There will be different dorms and classes for children with different animals, your dorm name is "kitty crown", You will have a room to yourself and there will be a common room where the people from your crown-which is another name for dormitory- will meet, I read this all in the other letters" Her mom explained

"Oh, really nice, I wonder how they have designed the rooms-"

Her mom interrupted

"They have a library, vets, laboratory, cafeteria, stables, cat stays, playgrounds, pet spas and so much more, Aurora you are indeed lucky to have an admission there"

Aurora nodded.

the car skidded to a halt in front of a building with a board reading:

PET ADOPTION ANIMAL SHELTER

"Here we are" Dad said

Aurora and her parents got out, there were some people around. All chatting excitedly.

They went to the receptionist who pointed them to a door with a board reading:

Cat and kitty adoption

The family of three went inside and Aurora gasped as she saw cages all around her, with cats of all colours and sizes, they had a litter box, a neat white blanket and food and water bowls. Some were kittens, some were adults. Aurora walked admiring the cats, the cages had cards attached to them giving basic information about the cat it hosted.

One pretty kitten caught her attention, it was white with pretty blue eyes, she read the information card

INFO CARD

Gender: Female

Breed: American Shorthair

Coat colour: White

Temperament: Sweet and demanding

There was the price too.

"I will name you pearl" She whispered as she put her hand on the cage. The 6-month-old kitten came to her hand, smelled it and meowed, looking at her, and that was the moment she knew that this kitten was for her.

3

Reaching The Academy

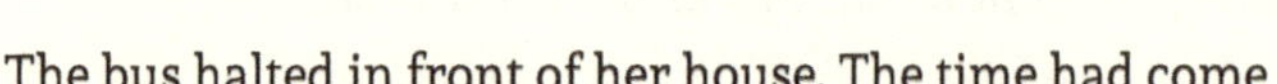

The bus halted in front of her house. The time had come

"Write to us whenever you can" Her dad said, hugging her

Her mom hugged her and said "There will be exiting activities on the weekends, you don't have to come every weekend, keep telling us the information you learn because we'll need for our own cat"

Aurora smiled and nodded, to her surprise, her parents had brought a cat for themselves too, saying they would feel lonely without Aurora.

Pearl meowed in her container that was sitting on her blue suitcase. Picking up the container with one hand and dragging the suitcase with other, she looked around and saw that there was a space under the seats to put the suitcases, along with netting on the ceilings to put bigger suitcases.

Aurora went to an empty seat and pushed her bag underneath the seat and put Pearl's container on her lap.

She looked out of the window at hedges, gardens, kids playing and houses passing by. The bus stopped in front of a house with neat roses in the gardens. A girl with blonde hair and light green eyes was waiting in the porch with her parents.

The girl came in and looked around for an empty seat, her eyes rested on the seat that was joined with Aurora.

With some difficulty, Aurora and the girl hauled her bag in the netting. Then the both girls settled down in their respective seats.

"My name is Ivy green, I have a pet cat I named Ginger"

Aurora smiled at Ivy, she seemed nice

"Nice name, My name is Aurora Stargaze, I also have a pet cat named Pearl"

"Since we both have cats, I suppose we will be in kitty crown" Ivy replied

Both were silent for a few minutes until a girl in the seat directly behind them said

"My name is Emily brown! I have a dog"

"What breed?" Ivy asked

"Poodle" Emily replied

Some other girls introduced themselves. And then they talked amongst themselves

"From how much time do you have Pearl?" Ivy asked Aurora

"Oh! Only from yesterday, we adopted her from a pet shelter, my parents also brought themselves a cat"

"Oh, very nice, Ginger belonged to my sister from 1 month, then when I got the admission to pet academy, she said I better take ginger there because she really didn't like taking care of him, he is 7 months old" Ivy explained

"Oh, what species is he! Mine is American shorthair and she is pure white, she is 6 months old"

"Mine is also American shorthair and he is orange"

During the journey, both girls chatted about cats and pets, Aurora realized that Ivy was very easy to be friends with, she found out the Ivy's favourite colour was green, favourite animal was wolf ("Oh!" Aurora said, "My favourite animal is also wolf and favourite colour is blue") Ivy didn't have lots of friends and she loved to read, just like Aurora.

"I think we have reached" A girl named Mia said, she had a rabbit.

Sure enough, the bus halted in front of a big building with a banner

"Welcome to Pet Academy"

4

Settling In

Aurora looked around, there was the riding arena to her left, though it was far away, in front of her were the crown buildings. She also saw the small animal clinic, the animal stays, and the library.

All the children were chatting excitedly, their animals were also making a noise.

A small van halted and 6 girls stepped out.

"They are the horse owners, they come in a different van, the horse transportation vehicle will be coming soon" Ivy whispered to Aurora

A proud looking girl with gorgeous red hair bumped into Aurora's arm

"Ow!" Aurora cried

"Hey! Watch your step" Ivy growled to the girl.

The red haired didn't stop.

"Cat owners, please stand near the cat stays, horse owners, please go to the stables, dog owners, go to the dog kennels, rabbit owners, go to the rabbit holes." a voice called out in a mike.

Kennels, stables, holes and Stays were the name of different buildings.

Dragging her bag with one hand and holding pearl's container with another, Aurora followed a herd of girls who were going towards the cat stays, Ivy was right behind Aurora.

There a women greeted them

"Helllooo my lovely cat lovers, I am Anna, Your cat helper, I will help your cat settle and also help you with different aspects, any questions?"

A girl named Leila said

"Hello miss Anna, I am Leila , I was wondering how this cat stay works"

"Oh well, your cats will have different rooms, you lovelies will take a bed, food bowls, litter trays, toys and all the other things for your cat in the cat store, then you will go to the room number assigned to your cat and place all those things, right now let me give you your identity cards and your pet's identity cards"

Anna handed each girl a packet containing two cards, Aurora opened hers and looked at Pearl's card

Species: American shorthair

Name: Pearl

Belonging to: Aurora Stargaze

Room number: 3

Aurora's room number was 4, in crown dormitory.

"So we keep our cats there when we are busy, they will be present in most of our lessons, can't we bring them in our rooms?" Ivy asked

"Next week you can bring them to your rooms, in weekends you and your cat can sleep in your room, kinda like a sleepover, And yes Ivy, You are right" Anna replied

The girls left their suitcases outside and went inside the cat stay, they followed anna to a section named: Cat store

Ivy took a green blanket, Aurora took a blue blanket, then they both took identical soft pretty pillow beds. They then took some food bowls and toys and went into their cat rooms

"Do you want me to help you with Pearl's room" Ivy asked

"Yes ofcourse" Aurora said, She had begun to like Ivy's presence

They went into the cat rooms and Aurora opened room number three and let pearl out of the container

"Wow, look at that cat tree" Ivy gasped

Aurora nodded, there were some ladders and wooden planks joined togather to make a nice climb for Pearl.

Pearl climbed to the lowest one and stretched

Ivy fitted the scratching post in one side, while Aurora spread out blankets and made the pillow bed comfortable. She then filled the food bowl with cat food Anna had handed out, and water in the other.

There were also some drawers in which there were some cat brushes, some cat treats and a ball. Aurora put the Cat identity card inside it too.

"Purr-fect" Ivy joked

Aurora laughed

5
First Impressions

After Aurora had helped Ginger settle down, She decided to meet other cats and their owners

"Oh hello! I am Elsa, I have a black British shorthair named panther"

Elsa and Panther matched in every way, Elsa's hair and eyes were glossy shining black just like panther's fur.

"Hi! My name is violet, I have a blue British shorthair named sky"

"Sky's coat matches your name" Ivy said to violet

After some more introductions, Aurora soon finds out that there are 6 girls in her crown.

Aurora, Ivy, Elsa, Violet and two more girls head back to their rooms, dragging the bags behind them.

A teacher greeted them

"I am your dorm's teacher; I will be the teacher of your most classes. You can call me Miss. Kacy"

Miss Kacy leads them to the Kitty crown, they passed the pony crown, bunny crown and puppy crown.

"This is your common room, where the girls of your dorm will meet togather" Miss Kacy explained, showing them a big hall lined with cosy sofas with a big table in a middle, there was a window and a balcony too. The Kitty common room was decorated with pictures, paintings and even had a small shelf with some books. It had some stools with flowers for design. On a wall there was a cat tree

"Sometimes when you will bring your cats here, they can play in that cat tree" Miss Kacy explained further

She then showed them the kitchen

"You will be eating dinner in your dormitory, everything will be cooked, you just have to bring it out"

Ivy nodded and Smiled at Aurora, Aurora smiled back shyly

Then Kacy showed the girls their rooms

"See, My room number is 3, yours is 4, we will be like neighbours, you want me to help you unpack?" Ivy asked

Aurora nodded and opened her room, Ivy gasped

The whole room was painted blue, the wallpaper was on the lower walls, light blue with pretty flowers.

There was a bed in the between of the room. It had some fluffy cat teddy bears and a really pretty pillow, the bedsheets were spread out nicely.

The whole room was lined with fluffy purple mattresses. there was a study table in front of a window, just next to the window was a balcony door. There was another door marked "Restroom"

The room was decorated with cat pictures, quotes, stickers and glitter, there was a bedside table with a lamp and some drawers.

There were some vases in small stools, and on the study table were some stationary stuff. There were some cabinets

"Oh. My. Gawd. Really! How'd they know your favourite colour? and look at that book shelf!" Ivy squealed

Aurora had missed the book shelf, there was an empty row and the other rows were filled with academy related books.

"Let's get to unpack"

Ivy took out the school syllabus books and lined them in the book shelf while Aurora opened the cabinets to find some t-shirts and other stuff. She then hanged her own clothes.

Aurora then opened the bathroom and gasped again, Ivy followed her.

"Wow!"

There was a bath tub lined with toy ducks. There was also a blue towel hanging on the other side. there was a shampoo and some other bottles on the bath tub. A pair of fluffy slippers were on the mat near the bathroom door. On the washbasin was a mirror lined with white lights.

"Love this, I am unpacked, want me to help you?" Aurora asked

"Yeah please, I am Dying to see what's in my room"

On their way out, Aurora wrote her name on the door and put some stickers around.

Ivy's room was a bit same, except everything was green.

"You know, Ivy is also a name for a type of a vine, that's why I like green."

"Oh" Aurora replied

They unpacked and kept talking, until there was a knock at the door.

"Hey, I am Elsa, remember me? We met at the cat stay" Elsa said as Ivy opened the room.

Aurora remembered panther and the black hair.

"Yes, what brings you here?" Ivy said

"The academy tour will start in 20 minutes, you guys better get ready, Miss Kacy told me that the coats in your cabinets with cat paw design is like a crown vest which will tell teachers from which crown you are"

"Oh! Then I must head back to my room" Aurora said

"And check your cabinet and bedside table drawers too" Elsa said

Elsa went to the common room, Ivy closed the door and Aurora went back to room number 4.

She took a pretty blue frock and hurried in the bathroom for a shower. She combed her silver hair and wore a hair clip, she slid down a small blue bracelet on her hands, then she took the Kitty crown vest and saw a small cat face engraved on it, some words : Kitty Crown Pet academy circled the design, like a logo. The vest was white with blue, green and pink lines on it

She wore it on, there was still some time left so she flopped on the soft bouncy bed.

Aurora then remembered the bedside table drawer, she opened it finding a schedule, for today she read

Monday 11 March

School Tour by Victoria Avanda: 1:30 P.m.

Lunch: 3 P.M. In the cafeteria

Tips for Cat Care: By Miss Kacy. Location: Cat classrooms. Things needed: Tips for cat care and your cat. Time: 4:30

English class: By Miss Clove, Location: Normal classes. Things needed: Basic grammar book. Time: 5: 30

That was it, tomorrow she saw they would have wildlife handling and research sessions.

It's all going to be very interesting she thought.

Victoria was a familiar name Aurora searched her memory for it... The sign on the letter! The principal name is Miss. Victoria!

6

The School

"Ok Young ladies, we will start the school tour from the library" All of the school students were gathered in front of the library. Kitty crown was huddled togather and Ivy held Aurora's hand.

They were met with the librarian.

"That section is about cats, that one is about dogs, to the left is the rabbit, just with it is about the birds, and in front is about horses, the last one has books on other things like wildlife, plants, weather and some others" She explained

Most of the kitty crown went to the Cat section, there were cat care tips, cat novels and literally everything about cats.

After the library Miss. Victoria showed them the mini playground for the students to play, it also had some swings and slides.

After that, they visited the wildlife centre where she would be having her wildlife care and handling session tomorrow, they had exotic birds and animals.

In the riding arena they were to learn horse riding, the horse owners would have riding sessions everyday on their horses, the school only had 6 extra horses so every day different crowns would use those horses to ride and learn.

They visited the pet spa in which they would be learning how to groom their animals, also there the animals could have proper baths.

Victoria showed them the Science lab, the sport club where kids could play different sports.

Now it was time for lunch.

The students went to the cafeteria, there were some serving counters and 5 tables for each crown. With Ivy by her side, Aurora went to the 'starter' counter and stood in the line

"Chocolate muffin, cheese sandwiches, Red pasta, noodles... Yum, you can only choose one of these" Ivy mumbled into Aurora's ear

"I am taking red pasta, you?" Aurora asked

"I think... cheese sandwich, we can both share"

"Okay"

After they ate the starters, they went into the main menu serving counter where Aurora took cheese burger while Ivy chose a taco.

For desert Aurora and Ivy both took chocolate pastries, and for beverages chocolate milkshakes.

"Now kids! Go feed your cats, Tomorrow you will be serving your pets first." A teacher said and continued "After that go to your classrooms"

Aurora nodded, she had a notebook, a pencil and the book in her side bag, Ivy also had one, they only had to fetch and feed their cats.

"Pearl! I am back!" Aurora exclaimed while she threw open the door of her cat's room.

Pearl meowed and circled her legs and Aurora bent down to pet her.

"Now let me see, you have finished your food... where did I put your food, yes here it is!"

Aurora took a can of wet tuna cat food and emptied it into the food bowl. While Pearl ate Aurora cleaned her litter tray, arranged the blankets and looked at her cat tenderly.

"I think you must wear a collar now so I can attach a lead to it" Aurora said after pearl had finished and then took out of her bag a pretty elastic blue collar with Pearl's name engraved on it.

But pearl hissed and backed away.

"Ok, I will have to ask Miss. Kacy how to make you wear a collar, I can't put you in the container every day" saying that, she put a treat in the container so pearl would come in and closed the door. Putting the packet of cat biscuits in her bag.

___

Turned out most of the students had problems with making their cats wearing the collars, so miss Kacy told them how to

"Violet? Please bring your cat sky on my table, do you have the collar and the cat biscuits? yes? good"

"Distract your cat with the treats then slowly petting the cat with your hands, slide the collar into the neck" following Miss Kacy's instructions, Violet easily collared her cat.

"Children, follow suit" Miss Kacy said

Soon, Pearl was also collared.

"Tomorrow you will go to the vet so he can check the health of your pets, you will also have the grooming class and wildlife and math class, now go to your English class" Miss Kacy said.

"We haven't got any homework for now, but in English class I'm 100% sure we will have to write an essay for a homework" Ivy joked and Other girls laughed

Ivy was right, they did get an essay for homework

"Ugh Ivy, what will be our tomorrow's homework, you are a homework predictor" Abby teased Ivy lightly.

The girls went to the cat rooms and took out their cats for a small walk in the playground.

Aurora Stargaze sighed with contentment as she lay down on her bed in her pyjamas, her day had ended with a tasty dinner and light jokes, she was happy.

Tomorrow she would write to her parents.

Ivy, Pearl, Elsa, Abby, Ginger thinking of all of the things she did today, Aurora closed her eyes and fell into a deep sleep.

7
Morning Surprises

Aurora was very bored, she had woken up very early and now was laying on her back on her soft bed. She tried to think of something to do, but everything was closed and sleeping, even Ivy.

I totally forgot about the cabinet and those more papers in my backside drawer! Switching on the lamp, she opened the drawer and took out the second and last paper

Rules

1. Everyone is to do their home works and assignments

2. No one is to go to the rainforest without permission

3. No one is to harass any animals, you might be expelled for it

4. No one is to skip classes and breakfast lunch and dinner

5. Everyone is to go back to their dormitories by 8 P.M. And not come out until 8 A.M.

Aurora then got up, opened her cabinet door and took out a box from the drawer, when she opened it. She was shocked. In that box was a new tablet, its cover had pet academy written on it. Aurora opened it and was met by: What is your name? Aurora wrote her full name on it and then it was opened, in there she saw some apps, all related to pets and animals. There was no option to download more apps.

There was an app to check the schedule too, she opened it to look up at today schedule

Tuesday:

Breakfast: Cafeteria at 8:30 A.M till 9 (Meet your pets at 8:00 and feed them too)

Cat Grooming: Pet Spa, By Miss Kimberly At 9:15 Till 9:45, Bring your cats and the grooming tools

Vet Check up: In pet Clinic by Doctor Oliver from 10:00 A.M , bring your cats and a blanket for them

Wildlife Care and Handling: By Wildlife biologist Sora, From 11:00 A.M to 11:30

Break: 12: 30 to 4:30 (Lunch at 2:30)

Maths class: By Miss. Kacy, from 4:30 to 5:20 P.M, bring maths foundation book

It was almost 8, Aurora took a quick bath, put all the books and essential things in her side bag and then went into the common room to find all the other girls

"Here you are!" Eleanor, another girl in her crown with freckles and curly dark brown hair said to Aurora

"Yes, Eleanor? Where's Ivy? Oh, hi Violet, your brown hair looks really nice... Where are all the others?"

"Well, Eleanor, Me, Violet, are here, Ivy will be coming soon too" Elsa said

"I am going to the cat-" "No!" Violet said in a loud voice, Aurora was surprised, Violet wasn't the type of girl who would actually shout, at least she didn't look like one, she was shyer than Aurora

"What, guys?"

"Let Ivy come first" Violet said. Ivy came after a bit, dressed in green, she also looked ready to go to the cat stay

"Hey! Wassup?? Wait, what happened to the happy faces?" Ivy said, frowning looking around

"We have to stay togather" Elsa finally said, sighing

"Because a monster has come? Guys be quick!" Aurora said, savagely

"Pony crown isn't nice; they are going around embarrassing and picking on everyone..." Elsa Begun

"So? Let's go to the cat stay! We can stay togather! no need to worry"

Aurora said, giving everyone a smile that told them that nothing is going to be bad

8
Friendships And Tensions

"Pearl! I'm back! Hungry? No worries, let's give you something to eat"

Pearl jumped out of her bed and ran to Aurora, who petted and kissed her on the ear.

"Let's give you dry mixed cat food with all flavours!" Aurora exclaimed and filled the food bowl with food. While Her cat ate, Aurora took the grooming tools, pearl's blanket, cat biscuits, cleaned the litter box and refilled.

"I will be coming in a while to pick you up, alright? We will be in those two lessons togather, in my free breaks I will come to meet you, ok bye!"

Aurora forgot all about Pony crown, she could only think about her sweet pet cat while walking to breakfast. Aurora was about to go to the serving counters but Ivy and Aurora bumped into Emily

"Hello! It's me Emily... Remember, we met on the bus? I had a poodle?"

"Yes, I do remember," Aurora said

"Wanna hang out with me and my best friend Jasmine at the big break?" Emily asked.

"Yeah, why not, I will bring my best friend Ivy with me too, but your dogs don't hate cats right?" Aurora asked, smiling at Ivy who smiled back

"No, I also have a poodle named rain, and he is very friendly with cats, Emily's poodle, Jewel is also very friendly" Jasmine replied

"Oh, that's nice, Lets meet at the mini playground after lunch, I will bring my other friends too" Ivy said

"Yeah, why not! If any of my friends have dogs who are friendly with cats I will bring them too!" Jasmine said

The girls went back to their crown tables. The kitty crown shared their food with each other, they had a healthy and tasty breakfast of pancakes, salad, pasta and fruits.

———

"Good, Open page number 171 and look at the brushes required for longhair grooming, for shorthair grooming look at age number 172 and look at the brushes required for shorthair grooming" Miss Kacy Instructed

Aurora took out a fine-toothed comb, soft natural brush and rubber brush. After grooming, the teacher taught about trimming nails and then she said to Aurora

"You've got a natural touch in your hands Aurora, Pearl is very comfortable" Aurora blushed under the compliment

Ginger squirmed while Ivy tried to brush her

"No not like that Ivy, be gentle" Miss Kimberly instructed

———

The girls laughed and played in the 15 minutes they had as a break, bunny crown was also there.

"Vet time!"

Ivy was second in line, Aurora was first.

"Hmm, let me check, ears, great health. Eyes, nose, mouth all great" The doctor did some more check-ups and said

"You have kept her in a tip top health, though I would say you must feed her different type of foods, here I am writing the menu,"

"Thanks doctor"

"Also take this multi vitamin drops from the pet store and moist cat food too"

"Hey I am going to bring these things before the wildlife biology, when all the kids have their pets checked then the class will start, other crowns will be sharing it too" Mia said, A bunny crowner

"Uhh alright, see you soon!" Aurora exclaimed, Playing with pearl.

Mia hurried through the corridors, her heart pounding as she cradled her rabbit. She could hear the faint echo of footsteps behind her, the sharp sound of sandals hitting the tiles. She didn't need to turn around to know who it was.

"Oh, look who it is," a cold, sharp voice cut through the silence. It was Valentina, the red-haired girl who always seemed to bring a chill wherever she went.

Mia quickened her pace, but Valentina wasn't one to be ignored.

"well?" Valentina's voice was now laced with a mocking edge, her presence like a shadow looming closer.

Mia stopped abruptly, her hands trembling slightly as she turned to face her. "What's your problem, Valentina?" she asked, her voice edged with frustration.

Valentina's eyes narrowed, a cruel smirk tugging at her lips. "My problem? My problem is you and your little group thinking your pets are something special."

Mia felt a surge of anger but tried to keep her voice steady. "I never said that! Horses are incredible, they're strong and beautiful—"

"I don't care," Valentina cut her off, her tone icy and full of disdain. "I can't stand girls like you. You prance around with your cats, dogs and rabbits like they're something to be proud of. They're for babies, not for real challenges."

Mia felt the sting of Valentina's words, her frustration boiling over into a tight knot in her chest. She clutched her rabbit closer, her voice shaking with both anger and a hint of fear. "You don't understand anything. It's not about competition, it's about caring for them—"

"Spare me the lecture, Mia," Valentina snapped, her voice dripping with venom. "You're wasting your time on things that don't matter. One day you'll see just how pointless it all is."

Valentina's words hung in the air like a dark cloud, and Mia felt a cold shiver run down her spine. She stood there, rooted to the spot as Valentina turned and walked away, leaving a heavy silence in her wake.

"Hey Mia the wildlife-" Aurora came running towards Mia but stopped when she saw her face

"What happened" Aurora askes

"Valentina" Mia replied in a sombre voice

"uhh"

"The red-haired girl, actually none of the girls of pony crown are bad, just her" Mia said

"Oh! What did she say?" Aurora inquired

Mia told the details

"Don't worry, she is just stupid to think that, I love horses! We must make friends with the nicer pony crowners, The wildlife sessions" Aurora said

"Alright then, I will just put Fluffy in the rabbit holes"

"Some girls are hanging out after lunch, the dog crown and the kitty crown, would you like to come?"
"Yeah"

9
The Wildlife Session

The pony, kitty and bunny crown were there.

"Ok girls, so in our wildlife centre we have exotic birds, animals and reptiles. I will be telling you how to take care of them. From now one I will be making groups of three kids and they will be taking care of one animal, of course I will be helping them. Violet from kitty crown will be paired up with Hannah from pony crown and Lily from bunny crown, Aurora Stargaze will be paired up with Ivy green from kitty crown and Valentina red who is from pony crown......" And she went on, pairing girls

"Ugh Ugh Ugh Triple ugh Valentina??" Ivy grumbled.

"Our group number is three, at least we both are paired up togather..." Aurora begun

"Hello" Valentina said, looking sombre

"Hello" Ivy replied

Aurora only glared at Valentina

They were assigned to a scarlet macaw named Luna, she had a big room to herself, it was filled with tree branches, perches and lots of other things

"Luna is really lonely, I found her when she was a baby and this place has been her home since. She can't fly because of an injury on her wings. No macaw ever plays with her, so that's why I paired her up with You girls,"

"Her favourite treat are berries, especially blue berries, her breakfast consists of berries, fruits, veggies and nuts, sometimes seeds... Now I will leave you from here, have to check on other kids"

Luna was sitting on a big fat plank and looked at Aurora, Ivy and Valentina attentively.

"Let me try" Valentina said, her voice seemed somewhat soft

Taking a big blueberry, she put it in front of her, Luna looked at the treat but still didn't come closer.

"It's a blueberry" Valentina said, her brown eyes looking at Luna.

After a bit of waiting, Ivy tried, then Aurora

"You want it?" Aurora asked in a gentle way, putting the blueberry a bit further away.

Luna slowly and cautiously came down, gripping the branches with her strong claws and beak, eyes fixed on Aurora's face, Luna took the berry and crushed it in her powerful beak. Aurora fed more Blue berries, each time putting the treats more closer to her body until she put one in her hand.

Luna stared at her, not the kind of distrusting stare, but more of a kind of stare people give you when they find you fascinating. Aurora felt a deep connection with luna.

Ivy squealed in joy and Valentina gasped when Luna stepped on Aurora's hands. Her heart skipped a beat then raced when she felt the macaw's light weight on her hands.

"How did you do it?" Valentina asked, her voice a little bit more than a whisper

"She is so pretty" Ivy said, awed.

Luna ate the berries, her gaze never leaving Aurora's face, vivid sky-blue eyes and silver wavy shiny long hair.

Aurora's silver hair was also something that set her apart from other kids in her previous school, they all called her 'grannie'. But Aurora didn't mind, she loved her unique hair. In this school, every student had different hair, eyes, colour, but no one was teased for it, no one commented on Aurora's personality or hair, not even once.

"Do you think Luna will let you touch her?"

Aurora's hands advanced towards Luna's red-feathered face and touched it lightly. Luna stopped eating and looked up at Aurora. She then again started to eat

The three girls sighed

"We did it!" Ivy said

Valentina came a bit closer and spoke

"Do you think...would it be possible...that Luna allows me to touch her?"

"You've got red hair and she has lots of red feathers, I suppose she'll like you" Ivy joked

"You could try, just be gentle, feed her first" Aurora instructed

A rasp berry was taken from the bowl and presented to Luna in Valentina's hands, without hesitation, Luna took it.

Then Valentina slowly stroked Luna's beautiful red and soft head, she didn't object

Ivy did the same and Luna allowed the girls to touch her, she was enjoying it because now she wasn't even eating, just taking those pats.

"Do you think she will step up on my hands?" Valentina asked

Aurora noticed that this proud girl had turned in to nervous flustered girl around Luna

"I suppose so"

Valentina advanced one arm towards Luna, who, with one look at Valentina, opened her majestic wings for to balance to show the vibrant greens and blues. And then she stepped up on Valentina's arm.

The door was opened

"HOW DID YOU DO THAT!" Sura literally Screamed

"Umm... I am very-" Ivy was about to say sorry

Luna squawked

"DO YOU KNOW SHE NEVER EVER STEPS UP ON STRANGERS OH MY GOD YOU ARE HER CARETAKERS NOW" Sura said fast and loudly

"Umm..." Aurora begain

"Do you want to be her caretakers? Sorry" Sura said in a normal voice and apologized

"Yes!" Valentina said

"You three will take care of her togather" Sura explained

"Yea-" Ivy begun

"Are you free this afternoon?" Sura asked

"Why?" Valentina asked

"I will talk about her care" Sura explained

"Sorry, Ivy and me are not free" Aurora apologized, the other girls could be waiting for her.

"Tomorrow afternoon then?" Sura asked

"Sure" Valentina replied

The lunch bell rang

Mia came running towards Aurora, followed by a horse crowner named Lisa

"Hey I Invited Lisa for the knowing each other hanging out, is that okay?" Mia asked

"Yeah"

Valentina was also there and she was talking with Ivy about Luna, Aurora felt bad about leaving her behind

"Hey, you busy this noon?"

"Nah, I think I will just go to my room or play with fire, my horse's name"

"Oh, would you like to hang out with us, after lunch? You can bring fire along, the other girls are also coming..."

"Me? Really, Sure why not... Hey, I just want to say, I'm really sorry about everything that happened between us." There was a brief, almost imperceptible pause. Mia and Aurora exchanged a glance, the memory of Valentina's sharp words still fresh in their minds. But then, Aurora nodded, a soft smile forming.

"We all have our moments. Just bring Fire along, and let's start fresh."

10

Pet Sleepover

1 week later

A week had passed, and it was weekend, and so had their real school year started.

Many important things had started to apply from this week, but one of the most important ones were Crown heads. The teachers had observed each and every student and made reports, the ones fit for this position would be made the Crown head

Each crown had one head, this head would be like the leader, they will be called to the important meetings, keep the crowns united, they can host parties and competitions, they also have to make reports of the performance of their crown, and a lot more.

"I think you should apply for the crown head role" Ivy said to Aurora one night, after dinner when they were sitting in couches and drinking hot choclate

"Me! No, someone else could be" Aurora said,

"I don't think I want to be one" Voilet said

"Yeah, you are perfect for the role" Leila added

"Really, guys-" Aurora begun

"You will be our head, tomorrow you will apply for the head role, after that will be the assembly in which they will tell who is the house head" Ivy interrupted

"Okay" Aurora had thought about applying for the head role, but wasn't sure about it... but now... she was

"This funny thing happened with sky today" Violet said

"Yeah?" Eleanor said, she had a yellow longhair who she had rescued

"So I opened the door to her room... and she was on the highest point on her cat tree, when she saw me she jumped towards me to greet me... and literally... she couldn't jump that far so she was about to fall and I tried to catch her but then she did a full backflip and made a dramatic landing"

"Aww that's so cute! Star and Me are bonding a bit, its difficult for him to settle here you know because he's a stray, so I let him out for a bit" Eleanor told her story

Aurora said

"And Pearl is so demanding guys, she just wants that wet tuna cat food and if I give her something else, she'll give me her best begging expression, and I just can't resist it, so now I mix up different wet foods with tuna wet food. And the moist and dry tuna food? She likes that too so I have to mix them up with the other types"

"Tomorrow we will be feeding our cats homemade food... I think we will be giving them an organic diet tomorrow? No cat food, maybe a bit of it... tomorrow we all have to bring some dried catnip and speciel cat milk" Ivy told

"You mean we would be baking things for them! That's so cool!" Leila exclaimed

"tomorrow lets run to the cat store huh?" Elsa suggested

"Yeah, I need to study about eagles tomorrow too because in my wildlife session I have a black kite to take care of paired Hannah and lily from bunny crown" Voilet said

"I have a macaw- WAIT what?! A black kite?" Eleanor exclaimed

"Yes, he's really nice actually...I heard from Sura that your group gained Luna's trust really fast?" Voilet asked Ivy

"Yeah" Ivy replied

"I have a fennec fox to take care of no he doesn't bite" Elsa said

"I have a turtle, don't remember the name! sorry not sorry" Leila said, smirking

———

Aurora had changed into her pyjamas and laid down in her bed, she was thinking about Tuesday, when they all had hanged out in the mini playground

Valentina had a orange horse, true to his name his fur was light orange and mane lighter orange, Lisa's horse's name was spots because he was white with black spots all over his body.

Jasmine's poodle named curl was brown, while Emily's poodle named jewel was as he was white.

Mia's rabbit was white with brown spots all over.

They had gone to the cafeteria and took some brownies for eating, after that everyone had turns riding spots and fire.

Curl and Jewel showed some tricks, Mia, Ivy and Aurora did not show any tricks because their pets didn't know any, which they were okay with.

———

"Knock knock hellooooo Auroraaaaaaa!! When will you wake up?" Aurora woke up the cheery voice of Eleanor.

"Yeah coming" Aurora replied sleepily.

She chose a blue T shirt with the photo an actual Northen lights shown in it.

Oh yeah! Today we can bring our pets into our crowns... And I have to apply for the head role, and we have to cat proof our room! Oh, my goodness...

"Guys! What are you doing here loafing around... Oh... Yeah, I totally forgot" Aurora said while coming out of her room, seening all of her crown girls lazing around in couches.

"Today is you and your pet day! They will be coming here, in our crown! Oh wait, WE HAVE TO CAT PROOF THIS PLACE" Ivy exclaimed

"Yes yeahh..." Leila said

"The best thing about today? No classes guys, other than the baking class of course, but still..." Eleanor said

"Yup, now let's make this place a heaven for our cats, let's go to the cat store and grab some things" Leila said excitedly

"6 cats will be visiting" Violet added seriously

"We need some nice soft pillows, cat toys, treats and what else? Oh yeah! Litter trays! And cat bowls, and blankets, ugh it's a whhooollleee list of things" Violet said, a bit sadly

"6 of all those things, wait I am making a list" Elsa replied

Elsa took a notepad from-who-knows-where and scribbled some words on it and threw it at violet.

"Oh, my goodness, we are gonna empty the store" Violet exclaimed after a look at the list

7 cat pillows (From the store)
Your cat's bowls, 2 (From your cat's room)
6 blankets, from the store,
2 big size litter boxes, cat store
Ping pong run balls, 3
Togather treat circle, big size (cat store)
Scratching post

Cat speciel milk (6 for baking class)
Dried powdered millet (6 for baking class)

"Hey, anyone has ping pong run balls?" Violet asked

"Nope, not me" Ivy said

Ping pong run balls were very bouncy and cats would run after them to catch them. Togather treat circle was used for lots of cats, it was like a circle and had different flavoured treat sticks on it.

"I do! Never used it though, we will have to bring 2 ping pongs from the store-" Leila replied

"Guys, we have to do the things fast before 12:30, the baking class... Let's go for some breakfast and then come back for arranging things" Ivy said

"Let's divide us into 2 teams, one will cat proof our crown and the other will take the things from the cat store" Aurora spoke

"I want to go wherever Elsa is" Eleanor said, smiling at Elsa, who smiled back. They seemed to have become best friends just like Ivy and Aurora

"Ok, Elsa, Eleanor and Leila will go the cat store, while me, Ivy and violet will cat proof this all"

"Fine by me really" Leila said, shrugging.

———

"Hello!" Yasmina greeted Aurora in the cafeteria, smiling widely. She was from the dog crown and had a white and black husky named serena

"Hello Yasmina! You seem in a good mood today!" Aurora replied

"Yup, everyone should be, our pets are visiting the crown!" Yasmina said, excitedly

"Yeah"

"Hello!" Lisa, a horse crowner said

"Oh, hi Lisa, how are you?" Aurora asked

"I'm fine... You know we will be going to our horses' rooms" Lisa told

"Wow that's cool!" Yasmina replied

"Yeah, when are you goin' to the pet spa huh?" Lisa asked

"Evening I geuss" Aurora replied

Ivy waves to Aurora

"Ok, Lisa and Yamina? Got to go!" Aurora said to Lisa and Yasmina

---

"Okay, team, let's cat-proof this place!" Aurora declared, her voice full of determination.

"First things first—vases! We don't want Pearl turning them into a crash course," Aurora said, grabbing the nearest vase and cradling it like a precious artifact. She made a dramatic show of tiptoeing to the cabinet and locking it inside.

"Goodbye, decorative plant. You were too good for this world," Ivy said, snatching the plant off the table and dramatically placing it on the balcony. She dusted her hands off like she'd just defused a bomb.

"Cables! The natural enemy of curious kittens everywhere," Ivy announced, scanning the room like a general surveying a battlefield. Aurora scrambled around, gathering up the tangled mess of cables and shoving them into the drawer, muttering, "Why do we even have so many of these?"

"Don't forget the chocolates!" Violet chimed in, pointing to a box on the counter. "You know how sneaky Sky can be."

Aurora grabbed the box, unwrapped a piece, and popped it into her mouth before stashing the rest away. "A little energy boost for all this hard work," she said with a grin.

"Uh-huh, sure," Ivy said, rolling her eyes. "Just make sure the kitchen is locked. We don't need a chocolate-covered cat incident."

After a few more minutes of bustling around, the girls stood back and admired their handiwork. The room was officially cat-proofed and looked surprisingly cozy with all the new additions.

"Well, that was a workout," Ivy said, flopping onto the sofa.

"At least we survived without any cat-tastrophes," Violet added with a smirk, making everyone groan at the pun.

"Let's just hope the cats appreciate our efforts," Aurora said, grabbing her bag. "Because I am not doing this again anytime soon."

"Hey guys... Brought all the things!"

Eleanor gave all the girls the special milk and the powdered dry catnip for the baking class.

Next, below the cat tree they put the togather treat circle. They spread the biggest blanket on the glass table, and some blanket on the lowest biggest cat tree planks.

Next, they put the litter boxes under the table, the pillows on the cat tree planks and the small tables. They lined the bowls against the wall that was the opposite to the cat tree.

They arranged everything

"Ok now, this looks great... Hmm, 12:30 baking class!" Ivy exclaimed, looking proudly around the transformed room.

"Yup, gonna grab my bag!"

"We will be meeting our care animals too, right?"

"yes"

Aurora was shocked when she saw Valentina was already there playing with Luna, Valentina wasn't bad, but she wasn't that good either. It took her time to get used to all this friendliness

"Uhh, hi" Aurora said, trying to get her attention

Valentina looked back, shocked

"Oh hello, I did everything so..." Valentina replied, trying not to meet her gaze

"Oh, that's nice, I will go to the baking class?" Aurora asked, getting the hint she wanted to be left alone

"Yeah, that's fine" Valentina said, shrugging and turning back to feeding Luna

"OK class, today, for your cats we will be preparing a delicious dinner for your cats..." The cook, Harris said

"Girls, there are 6 sets of everything you will need to prepare the dinner, please go and choose your sets" Harris instructed

Aurora stood with Ivy and saw that there were bowls, spoon, trays and other things placed in an identical order

"So girls, first we will be preparing the Egg dish, take those two boiled eggs and put it in the plates" He said

All girls took the two eggs provided and put them in the plate

"Separate the yolk and the white, crush it as finely as you can until it's like a powder,"

Aurora did as the cook instructed

"Done? Mix them up finely"

"Now mix it with yogurt until it's a bit like a cream"

"Okay girls this is it... now pack this in the tiffin I provided to take them back in the crown, return the tiffin when you can. Okay so we turn to our next part of cooking"

Aurora and her crown poured the creamy thing in the tiffin, it was a bit dry and lumpy, and yellow. But it looked nice

"The egg can be served as a treat; the main part will be this"

Harris asked them cut the cooked salmon in small pieces, after that they cut the cooked chicken and mixed it with cooked beans, he also asked to pack it in the tiffin.

After that, they mixed the speciel cat milk with powdered catnip.

"Girls, this is done. Our kitchen usually has all these supplies, you can bake things for your cat whenever you want. I will be teaching more recipes as we proceed into our school year"

Pearl meowed and sniffed at the tiffins in Aurora's hands

"Sorry we couldn't play much today, but today you sure will be having loads of fun!" Aurora exclaimed, attaching the lead the Pearl's collar.

From all the cat rooms, the kitty crown poured out with cats. When aurora got outside, there were dogs, rabbits and many children scattered all over the school grounds.

Most of the cats were Pearl's age, and so, they got friends easily. No fights, no nothing.

Abby's cat, lavender was a bicolour longhair, she had orange ears, orange tips of feet and the rest of the body was clear, her bushy tail matched with her fluffy body. She had orange eyes

Ginger, Ivy's cat, who was an American shorthair was like fire. His whole body was flaming orange with darker stripes, making him look a bit like a tiger, his flaming orange eyes matched his body.

Elsa's cat, Panther, who was a British shorthair was no little, he was as gorgeous as Ginger, his dark fur was as dark as the night sky, his green eyes twinkled as stars.

Violet's cat Sky, Who also was a British shorthair was very beautiful, having a dark blue coat as an early morning sky, her light eyes were like the afternoon sky.

Star, Eleanor's cat who was a yellow longhair was like the sun, his whole body was an uninterrupted yellow, with eyes just as yellow.

Pearl, an American shorthair stood out from the rest of the group, pure white coat as white as snow, pink nose and white feet pads, her eyes blue as glaciers.

11

The Pet Cemetery

The cats and their owners had loads of fun, and as it was Sunday, the cats could sleep in their owner's rooms!

"I totally forgot to cat proof my room..." Aurora said as she watched Panther and Ginger play fighting, Pearl and Sky had got on very well and now where chilling on a high, big plank of the cat tree.

Lavender was on Abby's lap, while Star was going around the room, sniffing here and there.

"It's almost 7, wanna go out for a walk with the cats? We will grab the beds and things on our way back"

"Yeaahh"

"Sky!" Violet called, Sky jumped from the plank and straight to her owner's feet

A tought came in Aurora's head

"I totally forgot to apply for the crown head role!" Aurora said

"Oh no! We will visit the principal's office too" Eleanor offered

"I will take Ivy with me; you guys can walk" Aurora said

"Yeah alright, the principal won't like 6 kids with their cats herding inside" Eleanor said, shrugging.

Ivy and Aurora walked through the cold corridors to the principal's office, Pearl was now on Aurora's Hands, while Ginger no longer was ahead of Ivy, he was as close as he could be

"Even the cats don't like this place" Ivy whispered, the corridors were so quiet it didn't seem right to break the silence

"Me neither, I am never gonna come alone here" Aurora whispered back

"Yup"

The icy cold corridor had finally ended, and in front of them was the principal's office. The last rays of sunlight hit the broken pavement and the small ground that lay between them and the principal's office.

The girls were crossing the small ground when a small hinged door to the very left of her caught her eye, it was not a lot faraway, the door led to another small ground

"Hey Ivy see" Aurora pointed to the door, stopping to a halt

"No Aurora, I am not going in there, I am feeling, well, a bit scared." Ivy said, looking around

"It is nothing, please just one look, if it will be locked, we will come back" Aurora pleaded

"Okayy, when I say we go, we go, okay?" Ivy gave in

"Yeah whatever." Aurora wasn't really listening

Picking up their cats, the group inched slowly to the gate. The gate was rusty and reddish brown, the walls were small, and only stood up to Aurora's chest.

There was a small rusty silver coloured plate that had some words

"Pet, Ce- Cemetery??" Ivy read it, with some difficulty

"Woah! The gate is opened, lets go inside"

"Uhh okay"

Pearl was closer Aurora's chest, she could feel her cat's heartbeat, it was pin drop silence

Rows upon rows were tombstones, big and small. There were pictures and names of the pet, also the name of what family owned it, and a quote from its owner.

"Hey, Aurora, look at that"

There was an old photograph of a white cat in someone's arm, it was looking up. The name of the cat was

"Pearl? That cat name was Pearl?" Aurora said, her voice trembling

"You were never found Alive" Ivy read from the tombstones

The cat was lost, but where, and why? Aurora could feel the owner's pain, waking up to finding that their cat wasn't there, she could imagine them looking there in here, because Aurora, also used to have a cat. She could remember the day clearly, when she saw him, on his bed as he was sleeping. But Aurora knew, that this time he was sleeping forever

She was missing him, right there right now, he was a lot like ginger, orange, but his name wasn't ginger. His name was Fire

Ginger would fill his space sometimes, when she felt like she missed him, and Valentina's horse made her see the name again, which was a bit hopeful.

She wanted to forget him, but the memories would come back one way or another.

"Aurora, are you okay?" Ivy asked in concerned voice

Aurora felt like she was about to cry

"Yeah" She tried to smile.

"Let's go huh?" Ivy said, she realized that her friend was going through something

12

Acting Strange

"She said there are chances I might get selected" Aurora said, smiling

"Yup" Ivy replied as they were collecting Pearl's things

"Do you think we should ask the principal about that cat?" Aurora replied, thinking about the gloomy cemetery

"Why? You looked sad; it would only make you sadder" Ivy asked

"That sad wasn't because of that Pearl" Aurora replied

"Huh?"

"Well, I had this cat... who- umm, well who died, he was really good cat, and when I saw that tomb I kinda remembered him... but that white cat hasn't got anything to with it, I want to know where that another Pearl got lost, so we can be careful" Aurora explained quickly

"Okay let's do it tomorrow, right now..." Ivy listened and spoke

"SLEEPOVERR" they both shouted togather

"WITH OUR CATS" they said louder

Ginger and Pearl looked up at them, with our-owners-have-gone-crazy look on their faces

"How do you like this place?" Aurora asked Pearl, they were setting in for the night.

The Night lamp was removed in the cupboard, with the cat pillow to take its place.

Pearl mewed and curled up on the pillow, Aurora decided to watch some vedios on her tablet. Closing the lights she opened Pet YouTube and watched some funny animals.

Pearl mewed after a while and jumped onto Aurora's blanket and buried her face in her silver hair.

"Whats up? Wanna sleep with me? Okayy, lets watch this first"

Aurora said while Pearl came closer and watched with her, after a while, Aurora's tablet closed and then she tried to sleep, with Pearl moving and twisting beside her.

Pearl Meowed and jumped up so suddenly that Aurora gave a small yelp, the wasn't even any light.

"Pearl, are you hungry? Is everything okay?" Aurora said urgently, she was feeling a bit scared

Aurora took Pearl and held her tightly, tiptoed and opened the night bulb

"That's okay?" Aurora asked, Pearl seemed to have calmed down

Soon, Aurora realized it wasn't the dark or hunger that was discomforting Pearl, it was that voice.

It was like someone breathing with their mouth, with lots of scary voice, tingled with an occasional hiss like voice, it was very low, but very scary and spine-tingling.

Throughout the night, Aurora's sleep was often broken by That voice and the tensed meow or Pearl. Aurora had ingnored the hiss thinking it was a pipe or something.

"Hey slept well?" Ivy asked in the common room, yawning

"Not me" Eleanor replied

"Me too" Abby said, cradling her cat

"Me three" Violet joked

"It was a hiss of sorts" Elsa said

"Like this: Hasssssss hisssss hasss hiissss" Eleanor said, intimating it

"Lavender hated that noise" Abby complained

"We will have to fix that" Aurora said

"It can wait though" Ivy replied

"She can easily choose someone else" Abby said

"Yeah..." Aurora replied mindlessly

"But I am a bit worried you know, how am I supposed to be handling all this?" Aurora asked, not really listening

"Don't worry, it will be okay, lets dress up now" Ivy said

"Crown heads are generally not a big topic in this school... My big sister also came here and she became a crown head, nothing really changed in her school life" Eleanor said

"That's good" Aurora replied, a bit relieved

13
Crown Heads

"Students of pet Academy, today I'll be telling the heads of our four crowns, dog crown, pony crown, kitty crown and rabbit crown"

"As you all might know, crown heads will be having more responsibilities then their normal crown members, it might be a bit pressuring, so if any of you don't want to be a crown head anymore you can remove your duties, someone else in your crown will do them"

"During exams, crown duties will be temporarily closed so you all can foucus on your studies"

Victoria explained on the mike to the assembly

"So now its time to announce our crown heads"

"Pony crown: Valentina red! Please step to the stage!" The teacher who was probably pony crown's said, there was a horde of claps and cheers and Valentina stepped on the stage, wearing a red wavy frock

"Dog crown: Emily brown!" Dog crown's teacher yelled over the shouts and cheers of dog crown, Emily went to the stage, to stand beside Valentina

"Bunny crown: Mia watts!" Mia went up to the stage, smiling and blushing

This is it Aurora thought, any moment miss Kacy would be calling out kitty crown's head.

"Kitty crown: Aurora Stargazer!" Miss Kacy shouted, the assembly erupted to a chorus of cheers and claps, Aurora, smiling stood up with Mia. She was having butterflies in her stomach because of the big crowd in front of her

Victoria held up a hand to silence students

"Your academic year has started, there will be classes, tests and a lot more, I really hope you will take it seriously" Victoria said seriously

"Enjoy your Sunday!" The teachers said togather, thus signalling the end of the meeting

"Not you head girls, stay here, we need to have a word with you" Miss Kacy said

The teachers led them into the same cold corridors, Aurora felt the same chill rise up her spine, though now it wasn't silent

When they stepped into the grounds between the principal's office and the corridors, Mia saw the Cemetery's door

"Hey, anyone knows whats that?" Mia asked

"It's a pet Cemetery" Aurora replied

"Hey, wanna visit it after the meeting?" Valentina asked

"Yeah"

"Ok"

14

Party Time!

"Soo" They had returned from the meeting, the principals

"This is creepy" Mia said, gulping around and looking at the tombs

"Where'd you get those flowers from?" Valentina asked, looking at some dried roses and petunias in Emily's hands

"That dried garden" Emily replied

"The principal needs to get her office's surroundings a bit more you know... cheery" Valentina said

"Yeahh" Aurora agreed

"So, because the day's free, wanna a small party for you know our achievement and the starting of the academic year?" Emily said

"Yeahh... lets organize it!" Mia replied excitedly

"So, our teachers talked about having one assistant or sidekick of sorts... Who are we going to make? Aurora asked"

"I donno, I was thinking about Lisa..." Valentina replied

"Let's go somewhere else to talk" Aurora said, looking around

Red mats were being spread on the grass, lights were being poled, counter tables were being set, a small table tennis table was being pushed to the centre, some chairs were scattered here and there.

The party was being organized.

The crown heads were running here and there and giving orders and suggestions, while the animal helpers were putting things, some kids were helping

"Hey Ivy!" Aurora said, running towards her friends

"Congratulations!" Ivy said, happily

"Hey wanna be my assistant?" Aurora asked

"Yeah! But I thought you would like someone more talented… you are not going to treat me like your servant are you?"

"Nope, you will be like my uhh, co-head or something, nothing much…"

"Ok I will give it a try"

———————

Soon the party was in full blow, ping pong was being played, some were chasing each other, others were showing their pets to each other. Some were eating, some were talking to each other and some were just sitting and looking around

Perfect Aurora thought.

It was like nothing could never go wrong again, with Ivy sitting by her side, she looked up at the setting sun.

If only she knew what was actually going to happen.

15

Exams And Creatures

1 week later

It was all great, being a head girl wasn't very difficult, but the studies were getting difficult

"How the heck am I supposed to do this stupid essay" Leila said throwing the pen in frustration, trying to prepare for the English exam, bended over the exercises

"Wait I will help you" Aurora came and started giving instructions.

The cats were mainly usually hanging out in the common room, though they would put the cats back in the cat stays when they were out to prevent any disaster

The exams would be over soon, the science one was this morning, tomorrow morning would be English and animal care and etc.

"Guys, what do you think about that noise?" Aurora inquired, when Leila was starting to get the hang of the exercises

"What noise- Oh... the one we hear every night?" Ivy asked

"I think It's really unsettling, I mean the school checked the pipes and all but they were okay" Violet replied, looking up from her work

Aurora had told the principal to ask someone to check the pipes or the gas line, but there was nothing. The voice would come everyday and would keep the students awake

"Something's fishy going in here" Elsa said a bit nervously

"The only thing that is fishy is this stupid essay!" Leila screamed

Eleanor rolled her eyes

"Wait, you do it like this" Eleanor went to Leila and gave some more instructions

———

"I think I absolutely nailed the exam" Elsa said, clutching the bag

It was evening, and they had come out from the exam hall (which was the normal studies- maths, English and history- classroom)

"I hope so" Eleanor said a bit nervously

"Don't ask about it" Leila said in a low voice

"Hey, it was a tiring day, let's go somewhere relaxing" Aurora suggested

"Yeah, and the weekends are coming up too" Ivy said happily

"This week was the longest" Violet retorted

They were going to the hallway and then crossed the notice board, Ivy gasped and pointed to a poster

It was a movie poster

"Oh! I didn't know there is a cinema" Elsa retorted

"Nope, I suppose they are turning the assembly hall into one, I mean I saw lots of chairs around It today" Eleanor told

"It's on 8 to 10! We can bring pets too; the dinner will be served during the movie... yay!" Ivy explained

"It's about people looking for their lost pets" Aurora said
"let's get ready for it!" Leila said

———————

The hall was lined with orange and red lights, there were different rows for each crown, with small tables in front. The arms of the chairs were quite big for the pets.

Pearl was wearing a pink bow and was staring attentively at the screen, Aurora sat next to Ivy.

The lights soon dimmed and the screen started to play, the hall went silent.

———————

"That was nice" Aurora said, yawning and coming out from the hall, there was a big end of the year party going on in the hall, Ivy and Aurora, not being the noisy party type went out with their pets.

They went into the park and walked around
"Can't believe our exams have ended" Ivy said
"Yeah" Aurora agreed
They looked around the park.
"I really like your dress, never saw it though" Ivy commented on Aurora's dress
"Thanks" Aurora replied
Aurora's gown was blue with plastic diamonds and pearls on the waist, the lower gown was sprinkled with glitter.

Ivy's gown was green, similar to Aurora's but was a bit more puffed.

"Ugh, the lower dress is speckled with dirt" Ivy complained

Aurora was about to comment on this when they heard a hiss, the cats tensed in their arms.

"Who is there" Aurora shouted, the only source of light being the light bulbs that flickered occasionally

"A snake maybe?" Ivy asked

"No, I have dealt with a lot of snakes and this doesn't sound like one" Aurora said, her voice trembling a bit

"Do you have a torch?" Aurora asked

"Yeah, it's a mini torch" Ivy said, rummaging her bag the equipment

Taking the torch from Ivy's hands and handing her Pearl, Aurora went closer to the source of voice, then suddenly the deep hiss and breath stopped.

"Is anything here?" Ivy asked, coming closer

The bushes moved and the branches cracked, something moved and shot into the forest, Ivy screamed and the cats tried to run away

"AAAARRGGH DID YOU SEE THAT" Aurora screamed and shouted into the night towards the rainforest

"We better report to the principal"

"Wait, I am going to sleep, I think we are seening things" Aurora said quickly, ingnoring Ivy she took Pearl and went out of the park quickly, with Ivy at her heals.

"Hey hey I know you are scared but you have to rest and eat" Aurora said to Pearl, trying to get terrified Pearl out of her hands, finally Aurora gave in and sat there until Pearl was back to normal-ish, she sat there and watched Pearl eat and then finally tucked her in to bed and closed to door, also she left the night bulb open

"The cats were really scared"

"Ginger too?"

"Yup"

The girls walk side by side to the crown buildings and opened the door, after some reading and talking they went back to their rooms.

16
Sleepover And Sneaking Out

Aurora was about to sleep when she heard the hiss, it was louder, urgent and closer. Aurora jumped when she heard a knock on her door.

"Yes?"

Violet, Elsa, Eleanor, Leila and Ivy were standing outside her door.

"We are having a sleepover; I am feeling really scared because of that voice" Ivy explained

"Okay" Aurora shrugged and grabbed her blankets and pillows

They all went to Abby's room, spread blankets and brought their pillows

Abby's room was pink, and pretty much her room had the same things that was in the other rooms, but she had lots of books, and the room was a bit messy too.

"Ok guys, we are all set and uhh a bit jammed, but still, let's get to sleep" Leila said, clapping her hands

"Hey, I want to have my cats back" Elsa said

"I forgot to close her door!" Eleanor squealed

"Me too" Ivy slapped her head

Violet smiled; her eyes shined at the prospect of an adventure

"If you both are going, then I am going too" Violet said excitedly

"I never broke a rule" Leila added nervously

"If we got caught, we will just tell we were worried about our pets" Aurora said

"I geuss... Okay so first we have to see if we are locked from outside" Ivy said forming a plan

"I don't think our crown door will be but the building might be" Aurora said

"I saw an emergency exit once" Violet offered

"That might not be locked" Elsa added

"Let's get some treats and torches, and let's go!"

The girls were yet faced with another challenge, the emergency exit wasn't locked, but Violet found out that if they opened it an alarm will ring out.

"Let me check the storage, it might have something of use" Elsa said, with Eleanor following her.

"Hey I found something!"

Aurora and Ivy went inside, in the middle of the storage room was a dusty box on which was written "Emergency" in bold rusty letters.

They unlocked the box with some difficulty and in it was a bundle of rope, some knives, fire extinguishers and a big rope ladder.

"Woah, do you think we can hang this out of a window"

Sure enough, the storage room window was big and had a speciel hook for hanging the rope ladder.

"Let me see, hmm okay even if we fall it won't be a big drop-" Aurora said sassily

"Oh, shut up Aurora" Ivy said rolling her eyes.

Eleanor gulped and looked at the ladder descending down into the darkness.

"It's our cats who are unsafe, guys you don't have to do it"

"And leave my friend? Never, oh don't look at me like that Eleanor, I mean my cat friend. Panther, I am bringing him" Elsa said Smirking

"Me too" Aurora said nodding

"Me three, though how will we climb up?" Leila asked

"Just like we climbed down, the cats can climb by themselves and our things will be in our bags, the cat things are ratioed in extras at our common room" Aurora said quickly making a plan

"Great! Now who will go down first?" Ivy asked, eyeing the ladder

"As the house head, its my responsibility to guide my crown. So it will be me, plus I have climbed rope ladders before, in uhh... less dangerous circumstances and more of a fun one, anyways, shine your torches down there, and hand me one, okay here I go"

Slowly she climbed out and gripped the rope, her legs finding the wood. The girls shined the torches down at her hands. Soon, she was laying down on the grass.

"Girls, be silent" Aurora whisper-shouted from below.

Slowly everyone was down until Leila was left

"Abby, you stay up so you can take up the ladder and throw it down when we need it, we will bring your cat. The teacher must not know any of our sneaking outs" Aurora instructed

"But I- Ugh okay... but next time I am not being left behind" Leila said crossly and took up the ladder and closed the window.

"Okay girls, follow me" Aurora whispered to the group.

Tiptoeing and hiding behind trees, under the flickering light of the light bulbs, they slowly neared to the cat stay

"Miss Kacy is there, she is on the night duty today, she might go away from here" Elsa whispered

"Maybe we could tell her what has happened and not get in any trouble?" Eleanor asked

"We will get in trouble, even detention maybe or getting expelled, or I might lose my post as house head, or maybe we might not be allowed for parties and competitions and-"

"Oh, shut up Aurora" Ivy said, yet again for the second time

Soon miss Kacy went away to check at dog kennels.

"Ok girls, its time" Aurora told

The girls ran to the cat Stay, which by their luck was only bolted, not locked. The key and the lock were on a chair, Miss Kacy must have forgot it.

They opened their cat's rooms; Eleanor took Abby's cat too as Star and Lavender were good friends.

Ivy came out of the room, on her arms was ginger who was purring now.

"Girls, lock the cat rooms and let's run out of here" Ivy instructed.

Clutching their cats, the group ran out of the cat stay and bolted the door, they just missed being caught by Miss Kacy by a few minutes.

"That... was... Close" Ivy said, between short breaths because of running

"Abby? Leila !" Aurora whisper-shouted from below once they were below the window.

The window opened and a big basket came down

"I created this as a small lift for the cats, put lavender and Star here! Only two cats per ride" Abby's head peaked down.

Eleanor let the cats in the basket, soon, all of the cats were lifted up, then the rope ladder came down and with some difficulty, the girls heaved themselves up

"So, what happened?" Leila asked Violet eagerly

"Oh, nothing much except stalking through the night in broken light, breaking in the cat stay, barely missing Miss. Kacy and then running through the night"

Leila crossed her arms.

"Oh, it was not that all good, anyways I have a vedio recorder and I recorded it all!" Violet said and handed her a small camera

"Do you think we should sleep in the hall?" Elsa asked, eyeing the yawning cat, her own Panther sitting on her lap.

"I geuss, Elsa, Eleanor! Bring all the blankets and pillows, Leila ? Violet! You both will take out the cat things from the kitty crown storage room, Ivy, you will help me arrange this hall" Aurora assigned

"Girls, close the lights! If the teachers see it they will come here" Ivy added.

The girls worked with the mini torches' lights, soon, the common room was a less like a common room and more of a cozy sleepover room.

The cats snuggled with their owners, and soon, everyone was sound asleep.

The next day was spent in talking, laughing and fun classes and activities, the week after this one they would be going back to home for winter breaks. They were having small revision classes, animal care classes (Miss Sura even gave them small missions to care for injured animals, calm down an afraid animal and a lot more, she even once took them with her on a mission in a rainforest to rescue some rare species of parrots whose chicks had fallen down from the next)

Everybody was having fun, there was no strange hissing and everything. The cats were normal and everything was normal too.

But little did they know that everything was about to change

17

Investigation

The hissing sound had started again and was disturbing everybody in the school. There were reports of missing treats, very scared pets and anxious people. Aurora overheard the teachers talking about parents being worried about their children. It these things continued, the school might have to close.

"Are you sure about the school closing?" Ivy asked Aurora during lunch time while the others were chatting about more pleasant things

"Hundred percent sure, we can't let the school close." Aurora exclaimed

"Yes, this has been the best school ever" Ivy said

"Hmm, then it is time for some detective stuff" Aurora concluded, finishing her juice

In their studying time the when everyone was studying, Aurora and Ivy scoured the sections of the library, every history book, rainforest book, fact book and even story books were thrown open and read hurriedly. There was no clue to what this creature might be, though Ivy suggested it might be a snake. It made sense but didn't explain the disappearances of the treats and scared pets.

The librarian looked a bit shocked at how the girls were reading books.

It was almost nightfall and still nothing was found.

The next day, Aurora and Ivy went to the library while the others went to the vet and pet parlour (Aurora and Ivy had took Pearl and ginger to both things on Sunday but the others were too lazy to do so)

They looked through the rainforest section, Aurora sat down to read a particularly interesting encyclopaedia. Ivy wandered of to the newspaper section.

"Aurora! I found something" She heard Ivy hiss. Slamming the book shut Aurora went to the newspaper section.

Rows upon rows of magazines were shelved. The smell of old books and dust lingered in the air

"What did you...." Aurora's voice trailed away because there. lo and behold! Hidden by a stack of yellow paper was a door with rusty sign saying restricted section.

"Well? What do you say?" Ivy said proudly making to move the paper stack out of the way.

"No, wait! I don't think the librarian will like us going in there," Aurora peeked behind the shelves and the librarian was sleeping.

"Well, we are safe on that side" Aurora said and removed the paper stack out of the way. They went into the dusty room. There were books about animal history never mentioned, horrific books about animal diseases, books about hauntings and lot more.

Ivy and Aurora scoured the dusty shelves, finding more and more dark books.

"Well, I am done," Aurora sighed sitting cautiously on one of the chairs.

"we can't rest, let's just look through these shelves one more time"

"You do it" but she still helped Ivy.

"oh gosh I found something!" Aurora exclaimed lifting a worn-out book titled "Pet academy's murky past" Looking through the content page the girls figured out it was exactly the book they needed.

They hurriedly got out and Aurora hid her book in the side bag.

"We are not really stealing the book; it a library book and we will return it" Ivy said much to Aurora's agreement and they arranged the old newspaper stack just like it was before.

Back in kitty crown, the girls flipped through the ancient pages. They found out that years ago pet academy took handful of selected students and did illegal secret experiments on animals, like trying to change normal animals into mythical beasts using painful methods which ultimately killed the animals.

The horrendous news was soon leaked to government officials who were under impression that the school did safe experiments, which eventually which eventually led to the closing of the school.

When the school was raided, the students had managed to develop a lot of hybrids, strange animals.

Most were captured and released into dense forests, but the most dangerous of them, a hybrid snake the size of an anaconda and ability to grow larger than most. It had venomous fangs; it was very agile and able to squeeze into small places. It escaped into the woods of pet academy along with a few more unknown animals.

The school was reopened by different people with a promise to lead young people into a good relationship with animals. The murky past was concealed from the large amount of public.

The snake still lurks in the pet academy forest.

Aurora and Ivy exchanged looks of fear, everything fell into place.

18

Points

"Hurry up class, only five minutes left for you to finish the test" Miss Kora- the history teacher -said checking the clock and writing something on a paper.

Aurora hurriedly flipped to the next page and wrote the answer to question num 14

What was the cause of black plague?

What was it? Cows? Chickens? Rats? Oh! It was something related to rats, though she had dawning feeling it was something on rats that had actually caused it.

Oh how much she hated history, miss Kora was ok though.

Quickly scribbling the answers to the rest of the questions she signed her name and closed the test file.

Ivy, who was sitting next to her said

"I have an Idea, meet me in the student lounge"

Aurora handed her file to the teacher and hurried to the cat stay meeting Mia on the way

"hello Aurora, how are you?"

"I am fine, you? And how is everything in bunny crown?"

"not good, our sushi keeps being stolen, the school serves sushi in all crowns in dinner." Mia said sadly

"But they stopped serving it!" Aurora exclaimed, shocked

"that's what I thought, but one of my Friend fond of the dish complained about it to the cook and they said they put sushi in our crown every day!" Mia explained

"So, it is being stolen in our crown too!" Aurora concluded

Mia looked around and said in a low voice "my friend's rabbit disappeared, apparently, she forgot to close the door of his room overnight, she didn't make a fuss and went to the principal's office with me. They gave her a new rabbit who looks exactly the same."

"so, nobody knows that her rabbit disappeared?"

"No, they have asked her to keep quiet about it. I know because I was with her when she found out the bunny disappeared. But please don't tell anyone except Ivy, if its important"

"I am so tired of this snake- I mean thing blundering around the academy, just take care of yourself and your bunnies, I mean, the school can't exchange a person."

Mia laughed and went away with her friends while Aurora walked towards a bridge above the academy's river. it was very high above and overlooked the school's ground.

Aurora loved this place; it had tables and comfy chairs. The sounds of water lapping each other and the wind blowing the leaves were very peaceful. Not lots of children came here because on the other side was nothing except a park so overgrown it was like a forest where miss sura often took them to birdwatch.

The out of bound pet academy forest started just where the overgrown park ended. Aurora sank into a chair and took out her journal, she had written her investigation points in there

<u>The Snakessssss Factsssss:</u>

- It's a cross between anaconda and king cobra (Would it have king cobra's venom too? Ivy reckons yes)
- The students called it king Anaconda, cool name btw
- It has a veryyy long lifespan (so that's why it's still alive)
- It's a male- phew, that means he can't lay eggs
- It's a carnivores, that's prob obvious

The Misssshapss caused by him:

- Bad sleep :(Ruined everybody's sleep with its stupid hisssss and that wasn't good for us during exams
- Scared our pets, Pearl wouldn't want to leave my side at night. She was slightly traumatized.
- Stole the fish from our pet kitchen lessons
- Stole the sushi
- Disappeared a rabbit (did he eat it!?Gosh, I should probably sneak Pearl to my room at night)

Possible danger alert: Could harm pets, even humans.
The Investigation

- King Anaconda Sighting: I saw him with Ivy but he shot towards the forest
- Meaning: A possibility of him having a house in the forest
- Stolen treats: Rabbits and fish, Sushi is also made from fish
- Meaning: Can eat all type of meat but prefers fish

(Could lure it in a trap using fish)
Cons And Pros in our investigation
Cons: We don't how it looks like, we don't have its photo either so we can't tell the school authorities or they'll think

we've made it up

Pros: We have a good lead into where he lives

Aurora closed her journal and opened her bag to put it in, catching a glimpse of her History textbook made her remember she was supposed to have met Ivy twenty minutes ago

19

The Plan

Aurora sprinted from the banks of the river to the student lounges. Student was a luxurious hotel like place. There you could book stalls to party in or talk privately. The rooms had tables, sofas and tv. The main hall of the student lounge had snacks which you had to pay for, but they weren't available in the cafeteria and were very exotic. It was only open on weekends.

When the beautiful building with a shining sign "*Student lounge*", Aurora slowed down, panting. She went into the building and there were girls all about, some with their pets and some without. Talking and laughing a group rushed past her making her feel a little alone.

Rushing to the receptionist's table she hurriedly asked,

"Is there any stall booked by Ivy Green?" Aurora asked

The receptionist replied "yes, Miss. Green asked to send in only Aurora stargaze,"

"Yes, I am her'

"Your stall number is 16.C, third floor"

Aurora rushed to the shake shop and brought two Choco chip marshmallow shakes topped with cherries, one had blue sprinkles (for) and one had green (for ivy). She hoped that this would make up to Ivy for being late.

The lift stopped at third floor and she walked through the deserted corridor ringing with muffled laughs and cheers.

Aurora opened the door of stall number 16. C. A beautiful room came into view and Ivy was sitting on a sofa examining her nails while talking to someone on phone. A box of raspberry donuts lay on the table.

"yeah, mum the neighbour shouldn't play the music so loud, anyways my friend has come so I will call you later"

Aurora sat on sofa opposite her. And Ivy said in cold voice

"Well, you took your time"

"Yeah I know that, I am sorry, I bumped into Mia on the way, and well.. it is a long story" Aurora kept the shakes on the table, took a donut and recounted what happened

"....and these are some notes I took" Aurora concluded, giving her the investigation journal and slurping on her shake.

"Hmm, very nice... in the cons, you wrote about we not knowing how it looks like, well if we see a 25- 15 feet snake it's going to be kind of obvious"

Stifling a giggle, Aurora asked "So, Ivy, why are we here?"

"I wanted to see this place; my other friends always talk about it. Its nice right?"

Aurora stared at her "yeah its nice but-"

"joking" Ivy said suddenly serious "anyways Aurora we need to capture it. I found ginger today in a very small box cramped behind the cat tree, and he was a little wounded"

Aurora gasped, "Oh poor Ginger, is he okay?"

"Yes he is fine. I took him to the vet and he said the it was the work night fright. But I reckon it's the work of the king anaconda"

"Oh thank goodness, and you are right"

"Did you not hear what I said? We have to capture it" Ivy said in a cross voice.

Aurora was shocked, Ivy was _never_ angry, and now... this. In a useless effort to calm her, Aurora said

"I agree with you Ivy, but-"

"Nobody gets it! Here rabbits are being eaten , sushi being stolen, cats being wounded and god knows what is going to happen next and here everybody's bent on pretending that nothing is going to happen!" Ivy said in a loud voice, standing up and pacing back and forth.

"Okay. Okay, we can do something about it, I think I have a nice lead into where the snake lives, we could go there tomorrow and take a picture of him" Aurora said in a gentle voice, barely managing to hide her shock

This calmed Ivy and she sat down, helping herself to a donut.

"But shouldn't we be capturing it?"

"No, not yet. Please I have a feeling we should go there" Aurora explained

"but isn't his den in the rainforest?"

"yes, I know we shouldn't be going there, but we will take the riding lesson horses, buttercup and Willow and sneak into the rainforest. I have golden paint to mark our way"

"okay, I am sorry about shouting, though" Ivy apologised

"its okay, I'd have done that too if this happened to Pearl" Aurora said, grinning and going out of the stall to go back to the crown, and perhaps to buy another box of donuts too.

20

Preperation

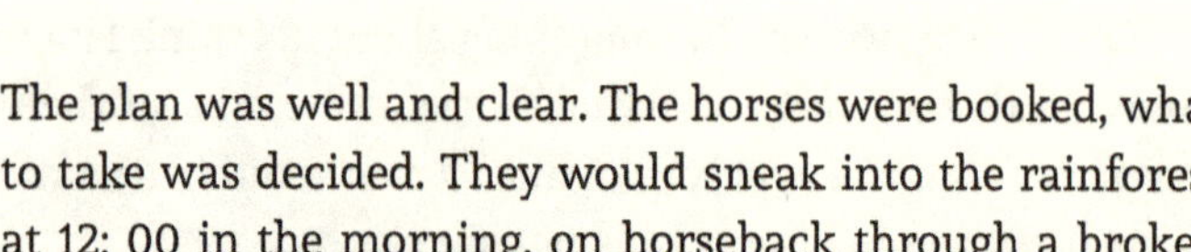

The plan was well and clear. The horses were booked, what to take was decided. They would sneak into the rainforest at 12: 00 in the morning, on horseback through a broken fence in the overgrown abandoned park. Then they would find their way to the place Aurora said the snake might live using compass

After dinner, Aurora went into her room and took out a shoulder bag and started packing on the list she had wrote

- Torches
- Golden paint (for marking their way)
- Camera
- Snacks (skittles and mars bar and popcorn)
- Water (a big bottle, with a bowl so buttercup can drink too)
- Apples and carrots (for buttercup, the horse)
- A compass (borrowed from Elsa)
- A mat (she didn't have one so took an extra bedsheet as substitute)
- Binouclours
- Notebooks and pen

- Field guides of the jungle (borrowed from the library)
- Pen knife

Zipping her bag Aurora took it and knocked on Ivy's room.

"it's Aurora!" she called

"come in!" Ivy called from inside

There, cross-legged, Ivy was trying to stuff another apple into her already full bag.

"don't make it too heavy, you're gonna feel like you are carrying rocks" Aurora said

Finally succeeding in putting the apple in her bag, Ivy lifted it and complained

"Gosh, it feels like I am carrying bricks" And started to take out some extra stuff

"It's quite late" Aurora said after Ivy had taken out several carrots and apples and a humongous bar of chocolate (which they had decided to eat after coming back), and gone through the plan again. It was almost 10:00.

Aurora went to her room and changed into her blue pyjamas with pink flamingos. She did her skincare routine and put Pearl to bed. She meowed and Aurora gave her some more cat treats, she thought how bad she would feel if Pearl disappeared like that rabbit had, and that's why she had successfully sneaked Pearl to her room

How she sneaked Pearl from her room- Aurora's point of view

I came from my room to the cat stay while Ivy went to a co-crown head meeting. We had to put our cats in their rooms before dinner, as 8:30 was curfew. If I wanted to do it, I had to do it before dinner.

I went into her room and found her taking a little catnap, when I came in she lifted her head to see who It was and went to sleep again.

I had a backpack and decided to put her in it. I would take her fav blanket, a packet of cat food and food bowl. The only problem was in the form of the guard, who by chance happened to be in front of the cat stay talking to Miss. Snootle, the maths teacher who also happened to be very mean.

But I am definitely not taking any chances against that stupid Anaconda, so I put all the stuff in the front pocket of the bag and scooped Pearl into my hands

"Okay girl, please be quiet if you want to be in my room," I whispered and put Pearl in the bag, chaining it only halfway up so she had air to breath.

"Whats with the big bag Aurora? Got something to hide?" Miss Snootle leered when I came out of the cat stay

"of course I have got nothing to hide," I said, smiling and putting my hands into my hoodie pockets.

"Hmm, then let me check your bag"

"Umm, I don't think that's allowed" The guard told, stepping up

"Shut up! I am a teacher; I can do anything I want. Now get out of my way or do you want me to complain about you?" Miss. Snootle snapped back.

The guard got silent and backed away. I took of my bag and hoped with all my heart she would only open the front pocket and ingnore the back one.

Miss. Snootle opened the front pocket and took out the blanket, cat food and food bowls.

"What is this for?" She asked

Quickly making up an excuse, I replied

"Uhh, I am preparing for tomorrow, you know, you are allowed to have a sleepover with your cats"

"I know that" She said angrily and marched away, apparently distraught that she wasn't able to find a reason to send me to detention.

But I was sure she wasn't convinced.

Back in my room, I took an old basket and made a comfy bed for her, which was practically useless as she was going to lounge on my sofa or the bed. It was almost dinner time so I poured her a bowl of cat food and went to eat.

Now

Pearl was purring happily and Aurora put the blanket over her head and slept.

21

Into The Woods

Buttercup and Willow were those horses that with one glance at them made you remember all the good things in the world.

Both of them were riding lessons horses and were as beautiful as the other horses. Buttercup always being assigned to Aurora resulted in becoming an absolute favorite. The mare had slightly brown body with golden-ish mane and tail and dark green eyes. Nobody knew her exact species as buttercup had been rescued from roads.

Willow was buttercup's sister, as they both looked alike, the only difference was willow had light green eyes and little bit darker hair. She was Ivy's fav.

"These are the horses, take good care of them. If I hear you ill-used them no one will be worse than me" The horse-riding teacher, Miss. Mellow said jokingly, as she always did.

Aurora laughed and said "These horses will be fit as a... horse"

She stroked buttercup's mane, tightened the straps of her backpack and leapt into the saddle, and so did Ivy.

They galloped through the school grounds to the bridge, Aurora felt relaxed and happy as she felt the cool wind on her face which also made silvery hair take a life of their own. If they managed to take a picture of the king anaconda, everyone would believe them and do something correct about the snake.

But what if they were caught, or something bad happened? Well, they had to save Pet academy and all the people and animals in it. Ivy was also thinking of something like that, though she was thinking more cautious thoughts, it was 25 feet king Anaconda they were dealing with, after all, not a mere mouse.

The horses slowed to a trot on the bridge, Ivy said

"you are sure about there is a broken fence?"

Aurora nodded, once she had wandered away during birdwatching and found the fence.

They passed the thick vegetation with some difficulty until they reached the boundary. It was tall, about height of a tall adult, there were wires with spikes encircling big strong sturdy rods. They followed the fence and Aurora jumped off Buttercup, took her reins and checked for some markings she had made to signal the broken fence was near.

They found it, eventually, a very big hole the wires and even the rods curling towards the pet academy.

It was a little gloomy at first, but then the rainforest showed its true colour. Fruits were hanging on the tall trees, flowers of every colour and size imaginable were hanging on creepers, bushes and even growing in the grass. Once the fence was out of sight Aurora smeared a tree with golden paint.

Ivy was having difficulties with willow, who was very excited and reared up at the sight of every colourful bird, which was often.

"Ivy, I think we should woah!" Aurora yelped as buttercup shifted into a gallop behind Ivy.

"Stop! Willow come on I will give you a carrot!" Ivy cried

Finally, the horses calmed down and the girls jumped of them, holding their reins tightly and leading them to a beautiful pond.

Lotuses and flowers Aurora didn't know a name of grew along the pond. A family of proud looking goose swam around, honking and quacking. Some kingfishers who were trying to fish timidly zipped away as soon they saw the group approaching.

"Wow!" Ivy let out a whistle of amazement.

Aurora spread the bedsheet on the grass laden with purple flowers, Ivy made the horses' reins long and tied them to a tree, the mares looked okay with it as they were able to wonder to the pond and eat grass.

Ivy took out some snack bars and Aurora took out the skittles. They both ate and drank water and Ivy tossed some apples and carrots to the horses.

After taking a couple of pictures of the pond and some pretty blue butterflies, they packed up and started again, but not before Aurora smeared some golden paint on the tree the horses had been tied.

The journey wasn't very eventful, except the colours had dimmed and it was almost evening. There weren't lots of colourful flowers either.

Everything seemed okay other then that, except for something they didn't know. Someone was following them, and they were really close.

22

Caught

———❦———

It was Miss. Snootle that had raised the alarm, she was already suspicious of Aurora. And that resulted her in wanting to keep an eye on her.

The teachers happened to be in the cafeteria during lunchtime, Miss. Snootle noticed the whole kitty crown was there except Aurora and Ivy. She told this to the other teachers and Miss. Mellow told them the girls had took some horses.

After asking around their worst fears were confirmed, the girls had been last spotted crossing the bridge towards the abandoned park on horseback.

A search team was volunteered and they looked all around the academy and the over grown park, not finding the girls anywhere they realized there was a gap in the fence and so they went inside.

The golden paint had done all the work for them.

After going a little further, Aurora felt the horses tense a bit.

"They've sensed something" Ivy whispered

Behind them, the bushes rustled and suddenly a figure burst out and said in strict voice,

"Aurora Stargaze and Ivy Green, you have been caught, do not try to escape or there will be consequences"
They both jumped off their horses and came to the group

23

Detention

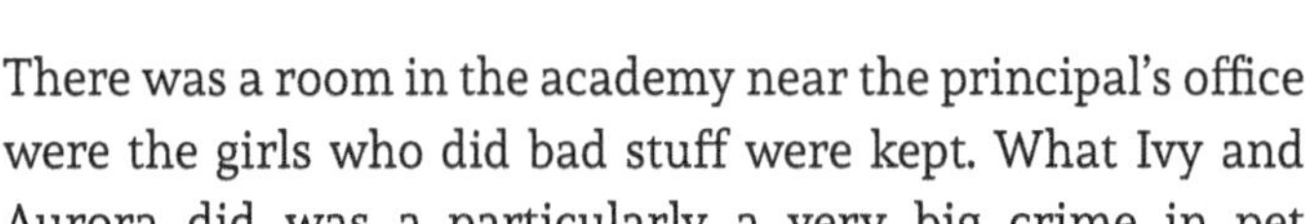

There was a room in the academy near the principal's office were the girls who did bad stuff were kept. What Ivy and Aurora did was a particularly a very big crime in pet academy, sneaking into the rainforest without a teacher.

It was a big room with grey sofas and tables, but no decorations. There were no windows and the walls were painted a dull grey. It felt like a prison.

Now as Aurora and Ivy were seated into one of the grey sofas, Aurora was burning with shame to notice everything was dull grey. Almost the whole school had seen them being marched to the principal's office. She was sure she was as red as a tomato.

Ivy on the other hand was staring at her hands, who were they kidding? They might be expelled for all she knew. No, This had been her dream school; she could not get expelled. If in not had been for Aurora... a red-hot burst of anger inflamed her heart.

The door opened and Miss. Kacy came, principal Miss. Victoria, miss Snootle and the rules inspector- Miss. Nais came in.

"Gosh. We are so dead" Ivy whimpered

Before Aurora could reply, the teachers took seats opposite them, miss. Kacy said

"Why did you go in there?"

"We wanted to-" Ivy was about to say the truth but Aurora cut across her

"To see the jungle... it was really beautiful, we saw... lots of stuff" there was no use saying the truth that would make them look crazy.

"To look? They should be expelled" Miss. Snootle raged, everyone ingnored her

"Were you not aware of the rules?" Miss. Victoria asked in a disappointed voice.

Ivy sniffed, Aurora looked at her and realized she was about to cry,

"Yes, we were," Aurora said in a low voice

Miss Nias then asked "You knew the consequences too, didn't you?"

Aurora and Ivy gave a shameful nod

Miss. Victoria took a deep breath and said in a voice that Aurora thought she was about to tell someone had died

"I am so sorry to say this, but_"

Aurora cut across her a blurted out the thing that had been nagging her

"It's all my fault! I took Ivy, she really didn't want to go to the forest. But I did... so don't punish her. Please"

There was a long silence and Miss. Victoria said

"As you both are house-heads and co- house heads we will give a second chance, but you will remain in detention centre today and come here again tomorrow. Aurora, you shall be suspended from house head role for two weeks. Elsa shall be made as a substitute house head. You both are banned from any parties that shall be thrown this month and are banned from the school parks this week"

"Urgh! She should be expelled" Miss. Snootle muttered as the teachers dispersed out.

"Now we are banned from almost everything and it's all because of you" Ivy said, Aurora looked at her, she looked furious

24

The Argument

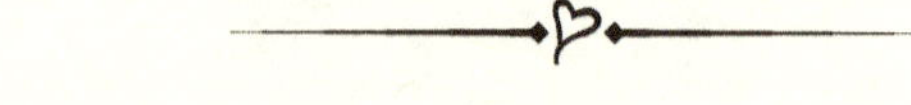

"How is it my fault?" Aurora asked

"It was you who said we should go into the jungle to get 'proof'" Making air qoutes, she continued "I wanted to capture it, you could have listened to me!" Ivy replied

"Oh yeah? And capture it with what? A bird cage? A watermelon?" Aurora snapped furiously

"We could have made plans!"

"This was the plan, silly, Two girls couldn't do anything! We needed proof first" Aurora explained, fists tucked under armpits, she was now starting to get really annoyed at Ivy.

"Everybody will now think us as disobedient girls, oh! And what about back home? My parents are going to kill us, and it's still all your fault"

"I saved us from getting expelled! You should be thanking me instead of accusing me!"

"Yeah, you solved your own mistake!" Ivy snapped

"Whats gotten in to you? It was you who ran around the room saying we needed to do something NOT ME"

"whatever, its still all your FAULT" Ivy replied, and with a flick of her blonde hair she went towards the far corner of the room, looking anywhere but Aurora.

I geuss I overreacted thought Aurora after a while *I should have been a little careful about planning everything. Ivy was just upset about everything, that's why she got angry*

Soon the day was over and the girls were free to go to the kitty crown. Elsa, Eleanor. Leila and Violet looked up as the door opened. They got up and Elsa said

"Aurora? Ivy? We heard that- "But before Elsa could finish Aurora swept into her room and closed the door behind her with a snap.

Inside Aurora sank into her bed with a sad sigh, Pearl meowed twice and not getting her attention she jumped and snuggled in with her owner, sensing she was sad.

Aurora sat up after a bit and stroked Pearl, gave her some food and change into her most fluffy and comfortable clothes. She then unpacked her bag (which had been left in her room after inspection) and ate all the leftover snacks and kept the carrots for the next riding class.

It was dinner time now but having ate all the snacks she didn't really feel hungry. So, when Elsa knocked her door, she tried to wriggle out of it.

"As substitute house head I order you to come out and have dinner right now" Elsa said in an orderly voice, almost laughing once, she also heard Leila giggle.

"Alright" Aurora said and got ready for dinner.

The table was spread with bread rolls, tomato soap, sushi, salad and pasta. Aurora let Pearl run over to the other cats who were lounging in the cat tree. Aurora sat down and poured some soup in her bowl.

"Ivy's not coming" Elsa said, coming from the room corridor and sitting down with a sigh.

"You could call her, Aurora" Violet said

"If I call her, she will never come to any of our dinners." Aurora replied, stirring and stirring her soup.

"Why? Wait, did you get into a fight with her?" Leila said, without any filters. Sometimes Aurora preferred it that way, tiptoeing around a subject never made anything better.

"Yeah, kind of" she admitted, shrugging and taking a bite of her peanut butter bread roll.

"We were really worried about you... what really was the reason of you going into the forest?" Violet asked

"yeah, we know you and you won't go in there to just 'look'" Eleanor spoke, making air qoutes.

"We are your friends; you can trust us" Leila said in a gentle voice.

Elsa nodded

"there's no use in telling you anything until all of my punishments are lifted and I make up with Ivy, but after that I promise to tell you everything." Aurora said getting up and going into her room.

25

Punishments

The following days were the worst days Aurora ever had in pet academy.

First of all, she wasn't allowed to go into the school parks, which meant no student lounge, no horse riding classes nor any swimming ones nor any wildlife sessions. The other classes were suited in the line of the crown buildings so sadly she had to take all of those.

Miss snootle's classes were far the worst, she took a great pleasure in ridiculing Aurora and shouting her mistakes in front of the whole class. Aurora usually gave her the silent treatment.

Whenever she passed other students, they would stare at her as she had grown an extra head or something, she was getting really annoyed by it. Surely, she wasn't the only person who broke the rules?

Even worse than this was when her parents emailed her, too angry to call her.

Not Very Dear Aurora,

We were quite shocked you pulled such a rash stunt. We could not believe our eyes when the principal told us about you and your friend so very irresponsibly. Did you

not realise how dangerous it is in the jungle, And you wanted to look at it, Seriously? Your intentions were very, very foolish.

I seriously have no idea where we were wrong in your raising. You were going well, then suddenly you went off track. You were never a rule breaker, now what happened?

In the summer holidays when you come home you are going to be grounded for one week. I hope you will understand to never ever do *anything* like this ever again.

Yours,

Mom

Aurora shut the laptop with a sigh, it not like she had been expecting lots and lots of love from her parents.

This was something she didn't understand, everybody was treating her like she had went to the moon illegally. It was not like she said she wanted a party, but atleast someone could say "hmm, you are quite brave". But no, if she did something a little unusual, everybody had to give her punishments.

And there was something even worse than this. Ivy not talking to her. Aurora never quite realised how much she needed Ivy; she was the optimistic funny one in their friendship. But without Ivy Aurora didn't just understand how to make plans to do something about the King Anaconda

Aurora got up and decided to do something else then overthinking. She saw the compass she had borrowed from Elsa laying on the desk and decided to return it.

The kitty crown common room was empty. *The horse-riding classes should be over by now. They must have gone to the cafeteria for lunch.*

She put on her kitty crown hoodie, wore her trainers, slipped the compass into her purse and went to the cafeteria.

The kitty crown table was occupied by all the girls, inculuding Ivy. She tried to slip out of the cafeteria unnoticed but Leila saw her and beckoned her to the table.

"Let me take my food then I will sit" Aurora said, looking at Ivy who looked away.

She took a choco lava cake, veggie noodles and orange juice. She sat down on the table; Ivy had left after eating very quickly. When everyone had eaten, they dispersed out, but before Aurora could go out Valentina, Emily and Mia stopped her

"You went into the jungle" Mia said in a serious

"The big dangourous jungle" Emily repeated

"Wow, girl. Bravo!" Valentina said, thumping her on the back.

"that is so super cool, I seriously can't believe it!" Mia cried

"We miss you so much being the house head, Elsa is very good but you are our friend" Emily said

"Thanks guys, seriously you are the first people to say this stuff to me" Aurora thanked.

They chatted for a bit and Aurora left for the cat care class, unknown to her that the kitty crown admired her and Ivy's bravery behind her back, as Aurora wasn't talking much to any of them.

26

Freedom

1 week later

The alarm clock ringed and tinged and Aurora sleepily closed the alarm from under the covers. Then she suddenly bolted up, today was the day not going into the school parks punishment would be over!

Rays of sunlight seeped in lines from the closed curtains, Aurora opened them and sunshine hit her. The weather was just like she was feeling today, clear, cheerful and sunshiny. She had decided to meet buttercup today and feed her the carrots, go to the student lounge with Mia, Emily and Valentina. Then she would try to make up with Ivy.

She got into her dress, a blue one which looked like a wave with silver lining of pearls on the waist and the neckline and designed her hair with a bow.

The king Anaconda had stopped bothering everyone, so she had stopped sneaking Pearl to her room, but today was Sunday so she could take Pearl in here. Oh gosh, everything was supposed to be going so well that Aurora couldn't believe it.

Outside, she walked to the cat stay and gave Pearl her favourite type of wet tuna food, groomed her beautiful long fur and let her out. Aurora didn't put Pearl on leash these days as Pearl would just follow her around

Back in kitty crown, Elsa asked

"We are going to the student lounge, wanna come?"

Aurora hadn't actually made plans with the house heads, she just thought she would catch them and ask them to go to the lounge

"Okay, I will come, is Ivy coming too?" she asked

"No, someone else invited her" Eleanor said. Aurora wasn't sure if she felt happy or bad about this arrangement.

In the lounge Elsa asked the receptionist for a large sized room. They got lots of milkshakes like oreo milkshakes, strawberry milkshakes, chocolate milkshakes all with marshmallows, cherries and sprinkles on top, to eat they brought raspberry donuts with chocolate icing, mini cakes which had all flavours combined and a lava cheese pizza.

The room had a humongous tv and the girls decided to watch frozen. Leila joked "we already got Elsa with us". Aurora ran down again to get some salted popcorn when she bumped into Ivy with the co-house heads. Lisa, Jasmine and Laila. They were buying ice cream. Lisa noticed her and waved; Aurora waved back to all of them. Aurora smiled uncertainly at Ivy; Ivy smiled back before turning to talk with jasmine.

Aurora's heart was almost bursting with happiness, soon, Ivy and her would be friends! Next Sunday they all would go to the student lounge togather. She popped a tangy popcorn in her mouth to celebrate and opened the door of room number 12. A, second floor.

27

The Snake's skin

Aurora woke up to Pearl pawing at her face, meowing and purring loudly. When she woke, Pearl jumped to her basket and slept.

These days Aurora let Pearl sleep in the cat stay as the snake had stopped bothering everyone. Putting books in her shoulder bag while Pearl ate some breakfast, Aurora left Pearl in the cat stay on her way to the cafeteria.

The school had given Aurora her role of house head back earlier then expected. As co-heads and house heads were supposed to be sitting together, Aurora sat next to Ivy.

The classes finished in a jumble of lectures, notes and gathering up the courage to talk to Ivy. The breaks bell rang and everybody ran to the cafeteria with growling stomachs. While waiting in line to get some cheesecakes, Ivy tapped her shoulder and spoke

"you wanna come to the bridge with me after lunch"

Aurora nodded eagerly; they would have roughly 30 minutes to talk. After hurried lunch the pair walked to the bridge

"so... Whats going on?" Ivy asked

"Nothing much, but... the king anaconda isnt bothering us anymore! Perhaps it went back to the jungle"

"Yeah, Umm, Actually I am-" Ivy was about to apologize

"Don't mention it,"

"No seriously I shouldn't have-"

"Well, we've made up now, it doesn't matter"

It was time for their wildlife session, Aurora wanted to meet luna and today they would birdwatch too.

"So, let's go to the class now" Ivy said

There was a little bit time before the birdwatching started so Aurora ran Luna's room, Velentina was feeding luna blue berries

"Oh hi Aurora" She said.

Luna climbed over to Aurora with a delighted squawk and landed on her arm, her nails piercing Aurora's skin. After feeding luna some berries it was time to go to the overgrown park.

"Hmm, strange" Miss Sura said in her singsong voice "those birds were supposed to be here"

The class was looking around with their binouclours. Aurora soon got tired of standing and sank against a tree flipping through the field guide gazing at the pictures of the yellow footed- Peigoens and the black backed woodpecker they were supposed to be spotting today.

Ivy sank against the same tree and spoke

"why is the park so queit today" Ivy was right, normally the birds would be warbling at the top of their voices and the squirrels twittering and everything. But today the squirrels seemed to be hidden in their holes and the birds perched at the top of the trees.

Suddenly, somebody's scream pierced the silence, everybody ran towards the voice. Aurora gasped and stifled her own shout of fear.

There, wedged between a tree was a snake's skin big as the biggest bus, with the width of a big sofa and the faded colour of the skin told one thing; the snake would be black the night. The skin could only be king Anacona's

28

Eleanor

It had been Eleanor who had screamed, she was crumpled on the leaf strewn floor and had covered her ears with her hands as if to protect them, Miss Sura ran to her and held Eleanor up, she had the look of someone who had been traumatized.

Leila , Elsa, Violet, Ivy and Aurora all crowded around Eleanor. The other students came nearer

"Oh my gosh, Eleanor what happened?" Elsa exclaimed to her

"Are you okay? Talk to me!" Miss. Sura said in panicked sort of voice

"I will call the school nurse" Leila said and sprinted away with two other girls at her heels.

Eleanor was soon ushered to the empty hospital wing. Even in her panicked state, Aurora noticed that unlike most hospitals this one had calming pink, green and blue walls and curtains and beds.

At night Eleanor was dispatched, the nurse said It was just because of shock. Because the kitty crown were her best friends they were required to coax the story of her shock out of Eleanor.

They all had a quite dinner, Eleanor was shrouded with a duvet and star was snuggled at his owner's feet (Star had been allowed with Eleanor for moral support). After dinner, Ivy and Violet brought a tray a steaming hot chocolate with marshmallows and a plate of chocolate brownies.

"Okay now Eleanor, were you afraid of the snake's skin or something else?" Ivy said in a gentle voice

Eleanor took a sip of her drink and cleared her throat, threw the duvet off her and stretched. Everybody stared at her in shock

"wait, so were you acting to be traumatized?" Aurora asked

"Yes, I wanted to tell you guys first. Though my pose and scream in the first few moments weren't acting" she explained, helping herself to a brownie.

Leila glared at her "you should become an actor one day, you know that?"

"Yes, I do. Anyways I know what has been causing trouble from the past months" Eleanor said seriously.

Ivy stifled a gasp. Everyone was hanging on Eleanors every word

"I wandered off because we weren't birdwatching. I heard a strange rustling hissing voice going towards the academy. I tried to follow it but before I could, I saw the skin." There she stopped and sipped her drink.

"I was shocked and thought it was alive, but then I came to my senses and realized it was the skin of some humongous snake. And then something very dark came in front of me with a terrible hissing. I thought night had come until I realized that it was moving. It was long and almost never ending"

"the hissing grew and grew until it sort of tranced me and the face of the monster came in view. I realized it was a snake with fangs as long as my arms and its eyes were a bloody red. Terrified, I came out of my trance I fell over to protect myself. I was so sure it would strike me and I screamed, when I opened my eyes, it was miss sura and you guys." Eleanor finished and took other brownie, her face looking a little scared.

All the girls around her looked horrified

"I think now is the time we tell you about king anaconda." Aurora said and brought her notes and the book. Ivy and Aurora both explained everything that had happened and what they had pieced togather

"We never knew what we were dealing with" Ivy said

"I thought it was gone" Elsa spoke sadly

Looking out of the window, Aurora said gravely

"But now he has come back, bigger and stronger then before. But we will be waiting for him"

29

Disapearence

The snake's skin had been taken away by the school overnight. Miss. Victoria had given a speech telling them the school authorities will take care of everything and to not panic. They asked the students to keep quiet about it to even their families because they didn't have any proof.

Aurora went to the cat stay sleepily. The hissing had kept her awake all night, in a flurry of panic because of Eleanor she had forgotten to sneak Pearl into her room before dinner. After curfew the cat stay was being locked as a precaution.

Aurora opened Pearl's room. The cat wasn't on the floor so Aurora's eyes searched the planks of the cat tree, nothing was there. Telling herself to not panic Aurora searched every corner of the room. As the full shock of what had happened hit her, she leaned against the wall for support, swaying with shock.

She then went outside and looked at every possible place in the cat stay's hall only to be unsuccessful. Then Aurora searched the surrounding grounds, knowing well enough she had skipped breakfast.

Pearl was to be found nowhere at all and Aurora tried to not cry like a baby. Ivy walked over to her.

"Classes are cancelled for today. Many people have lost their pets... A big search has started in the school. Everybody's volunteered. Where were you? I looked for you..." She trailed away when she looked at Aurora's face

"What happened?"

"Pearl's lost" Aurora sniffed.

When Aurora was too sad to do anything, it was Ivy who took charge. She was the one who messaged everyone to come to the kitty crown Asap and comforted Aurora, who felt a little bit better.

"She's disappeared? What do you mean?!" Leila shrieked

"Apparently she didn't disappear into thin air, the snake took her" Eleanor said, matter of factly.

"lots of pets disappeared today, so he definitely didn't eat her or any of the others" Elsa reasoned

"So, we go to the forest to find all of them" Violet said excitedly, her eyes shining just like they did that day when sneaked out to take their cats.

"He's not in the jungle" Aurora blurted, it all made sense "I pieced togather some clues. I think the snake sometimes goes in the jungle but lives here. Have you ever read about pets getting lost here? If he had a house in the jungle we would have have found becuase we crossed half of the jungle and if his house was further away it would take to long for him to come and go. He lives somewhere here"

"Oh my god. This makes everything even more complicated. It also makes sense, why would the snake shed its skin here when he had the whole forest? Answer, he shed it here because this was his home" Ivy agreed.

"I am freaking out." Leila said dramatically

"We need to divide into two groups, one will search the eastern and Northen while the other searches the southern and western" Aurora said

It was decided that Ivy would search southern and western with Leila and Violet while Aurora would search Northen and eastern with Elsa and Eleanor.

30

The Abandoned Building

Their first stop was the cat play park. They looked everywhere for any sign of the snake or Pearl, only to find none. They searched almost every park, and while looking in the horse-riding arena, Aurora had a text from Ivy.

Ivy: we've searched the pet spa, cat stays, rabbit holes, dog kennels and horse stables, the hospital... There are still a few places left. Any luck on your side?

Aurora: DUH, I am so tired... And there a few parks left still, you wanna join up the two teams?

Ivy: OH Please. And I need a break. Let's meet in the cafeteria and have lunch too

Aurora: Great! I am starving. Coming right up!

Aurora told Elsa and Eleanor about the arrangement and they agreed eagerly. On the kitty crown table Ivy said worriedly

"Whats gonna happen now?"

"I have no idea; we have looked at every place and we have found nothing" Elsa replied

"Well not everywhere, we have got the abandoned building, the student hospital, and a few more parks" Leila said, taking a bite of her pasta and studying the school map

"what is the abandoned building?" Aurora asked, trying to distract herself from Pearl.

"Very long ago, before pet academy wasn't even pet academy, the school wanted to make a very big and advanced lab. Apparently, the building was never made and the school left it standing because it was hidden behind the trees. You know, there are rumours it is haunted"

"I never heard of it that way, and there's no such thing as ghost" Violet reasoned

Leila rolled her eyes "Ye-Ah I know... some colour won't kill anyone"

Violet opened her mouth to object and Aurora cut her off

"I am guessing it's in the overgrown park?"

"Yes, I have been near the building once, I know where it is" Leila said.

Everyone hurriedly finished lunch and went to the overgrown park. Leila led them to a direction Aurora had never been too. It was strange somehow, like an unexplored territory.

The bird song had stilled now, and, they started to see strands of fur stuck in the tree branches. Though no one was admitting it, they all felt a little afraid.

"We should have some weapons you know... just in case" Eleanor said quietly.

"The building will have lots of them, it was a construction site once" Leila reassured.

They walked on until it was almost like they were in the jungle. It was becoming difficult to walk. Aurora parted a bush and everybody gasped.

There were only two words to describe it; Terrifyingly beautiful. It would be grey when it was new but now was almost green because of the creepers and moss growing on it. There were roots growing downwards that made the building look like it was alive. The windows were without glasses but the building looked like it was crumbling.

"Wow" Ivy gasped

"It smells though" Violet said,

She was right, the place did smell, like rotten eggs or something even worse than that.

"Before going in to the building, lets forage for weapons"

31

Foraging

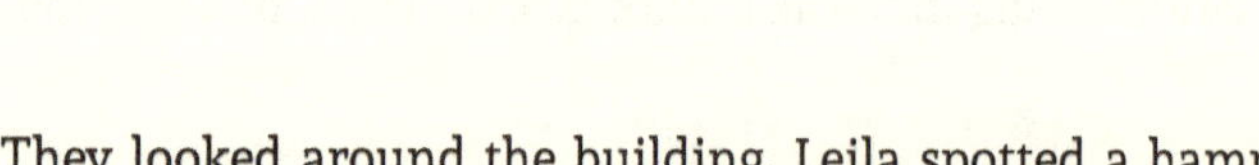

They looked around the building, Leila spotted a hammer and ran to it before anybody would claim it. It big a sturdy and had a little pointed end.

Ivy found a dagger-like knife and claimed it, Violet found a baton and made it hers.

Elsa saw an iron ball as big her opened hand attached to a sturdy chain and took it happily; Eleanor found a spear.

For Aurora they had to search around but found it eventually. For her there was a bow and arrow.

"Wow, it's like someone purposefully dropped this stuff" Leila exclaimed.

"Some of the stuff was used in construction and some of it might have been left here by people who come to explore" Violet reasoned

"So... shall we go?" Ivy gulped, looking nervous.

Every body looked towards the building and clenched their weapons tighter.

"Let's go" Aurora replied

32

Finding Pearl

They went in through the crumbling door. Inside was pitch dark, luckily Ivy had a torch that gave lots of light. Everything was silent, the only sound was of them walking. There was no sign of the snake, though the smell had worsened badly and Aurora felt like gagging.

"There's nothing in here" Leila said, resigned.

"Look! There's a staircase" Ivy exclaimed.

A rusting spiralling staircase led upwards.

"I'll go first, it doesn't seem like it will be able to hold the weight of lots of people" Aurora said and took the torch from Ivy.

The staircase creaked at her first step, but it held. She took the second step and third and went up. She then looked around and looked around, she spotting no danger she shone the light towards the staircase so others could climb up.

"oh my gosh, this was so scary" Eleanor said

"I get it why people called this place haunted" Violet agreed

"But nothing happened, right?" Aurora reassured.

They continued walking, now in pleasurably more light, thanks to the windows. They had stopped jumping at every small voice and were feeling a little more cheerful

Aurora took a turn and the rest followed her, there were no windows here so Ivy opened her torch.

"Keep your eyes peeled for any sign of the pets" Aurora said, thinking of Pearl

They continued to walk, now looking around for a staircase. Ivy was flashing her light here and there so much that Aurora's eyes started to hurt.

Eleanor and Elsa were whispering about something, Aurora was flexing her bow string and took an arrow from her quiver, marvelling at the sharpness of the tip. She used to take archery classes before she came to pet academy and had a good aim, but she still wasn't sure how good she would be in shooting an actual dangerous threat.

Suddenly, there was a sudden sound, like an animal walking fast. There were low growls and rasps coming from somewhere. The place was so empty and quiet that sounds echoed.

Aurora quickly loaded her bow with an arrow and pointed it in front of her, ready to take shot at any moment. Elsa pointed her spear in front of her and Elsa brandished her iron ball, ready to take swing. Ivy faced the back waving her dagger, Leila and Violet raised their weapons, ready to swing at any moment.

The growling animal came from the front turn. Nobody moved until Ivy, Leila and Violet turned towards Aurora and laughed. Aurora ran and swept the animal that was Pearl of her feet.

"Oh my! You are here! Oh Pearl" Aurora cried, giddy with relief

"That means the other animals are also here!" Ivy exclaimed

"We have to be more careful now though, this means the snake is here" Leila said gravely, breaking the happiness

"Urgh, you are such a spoiler" Violet complained

"Well, I say the truth" Leila snapped back

"Well, let's get going, right?" Aurora said, stroking Pearl.

They looked around on the floor they were in for the pet, and then decided Pearl had escaped from the floor above.

Finding a staircase, Aurora went first and gagged upon reaching there. It smelled so bad, like something very badly rotten. Pearl meowed in protest and leaped of her arms, going in a turn and looking at Aurora, gesturing her to follow her.

"Stop! Wait for the others" Aurora ordered, and Pearl, recognising the tone very patiently waited.

33

The King Anaconda

Once everybody had climbed up, Aurora told everyone about Pearl wanted them to follow her. Everyone agreed as Pearl was their only option.

This seemed to be the last floor, as there was a small peephole and all of them looked through it, they were very high up. Other then that, there seemed to be no windows. Aurora wondered how the air came in, probably from an air duct.

After walking for what seemed like ages (it was only five minutes) The path ended into a hall as big as an arena. There were so many ladders and holes and doors that Aurora couldn't count them. The smell of rotten something was so bad that Aurora almost vomited then almost screamed because she had spotted a bunch of bones near the entrance.

"We should probably go" Leila whimpered

But then they heard a faint hiss then a faint clicking. Aurora's heart came to her throat and she slowly turned around, followed by the other girls. Ivy dropped the torch and to Aurora's horror, the torch light stopped coming.

But they could still see the dark long shape, the glint of the dripping fangs, the gleam of the red eyes. A structure so terrifying that it only could have been the King Anaconda.

Thank goodness Pearl hid somewhere Aurora thought, her bow on her back, forgotten. The Anaconda hissed and Aurora's mind screamed her to move, to run away. But it was like her limbs had a mind of their own.

Eleanor jabbed her spear in front of her, by her sudden movement all of them broke out of their trance and they tried to run away. But in a small slither the snake cornered them against the wall. He struck at Elsa, who swung her ball and with a small thud it hit the snake's nose. Eleanor jabbed her spear on the part of the snake was on the floor. With a terrifying hiss he turned towards her, Aurora took out her bow and loaded it with an arrow from the quiver. Took aim for the snake's eyes, released the bow but missed, hitting the place above the snake's eyes.

If it was possible, the snake's eyes gleamed redder as he came towards her. With a high leap that could have broken the world record, Ivy brandished her dagger and sliced the skin above the snake's neck.

The snake hissed and made clicking noises and suddenly slithered away, leaving the girls shocked.

"everyone, form a circle" Aurora screamed and they formed a circle, each girl ready with her weapon and facing a different direction.

"Where is he?" Ivy asked to no one worriedly

"Perhaps he gave up" Leila said hopefully.

Aurora doubted it, that seemed too easy. A drop landed on her clothes, she brushed it away, then another, she brushed it away again. when another fell Aurora looked up and screamed, for the king anaconda was hanging upside down, poised to strike at any moment.

34

The Final Showdown

The girls ran away screaming from under the snake, like a nightmare the snake jumped down and slithered to the girls. This time they were ready to fight, but the king anaconda was like night itself.

He had seemed to take a great dislike to Aurora, as he was working very hard to separate her from the group. Finally, he succeeded and Aurora found herself running in the opposite direction from her group.

Aurora quickly pointed her loaded bow at the snake's eyes and tried to take aim. She released and her plan worked! The snake's eye was arrowed and that gave Aurora some time to run away.

"He's gonna be busy with his eye now, come on, let's find the pets" Aurora cried and they all ran from the arena.

Suddenly, As Elsa opened another room to investigate, the girls found that one was also a big arena but with windows. Pearl jumped into step behind Aurora.

"Hey! Where did you come from? Please stay hidden" Aurora said

But Pearl was again trying to lead them to the arena where the snake was

"The pets are there" Ivy said

"Can't we call the school or something?" Leila asked

"No, we can't trust the school with this" Eleanor said

"They'll probably kill us to hide their secret" Violet agreed

The girls decided to look for the pet's more but when they turned, they saw the snake silhouetted at the entrance, creeping up to them.

Ivy gave a wild cry and everybody followed her, bearing on the snake, who just crawled up the wall, his one eye bloodstained. He tried to jump on all of them but missed, as the girls were quite fast.

Slithering fast he circled his body around Aurora in a way that she was trapped.

"She's trapped!" Someone shouted

With a flick of his monstruous tail the snake hit her friends at once and they all went flying with the force of the flick. Atleast they were alive.

Aurora could see the great red eyes of the snake. The glint of his fangs, he drew his head back,he was about to strike her. Aurora couldn't move no matter how much her body screamed to move.

Something white suddenly sprinted on the long body of the snake and attacked his head, biting it so tightly that the snake started to flung his head here and there, loosening his grip on Aurora and giving her a chance to escape.

Aurora realized that it was Pearl who had attacked the snake, who was finally able to throw her off. Aurora barely caught the half- conscious cat and thought about all the losses the snake had given. she gave Pearl to Ivy and with a burst of red-hot fury, she decided to fight the King Anaconda.

The snake advanced towards the girl, who loaded her bow and took aim for the snake's neck. She launched the arrow which missed the snake entirely. Aurora launched arrows upon arrows, running along the arena, the anaconda following her like a shadow.

But soon she was cornered, Aurora tried to launch another arrow but found she had ran out of them.

"Oh what the…" She muttered and prayed there would be some of her left to bury.

"Aurora!" Someone shouted and there was a sword hurled at her. Before she knew it she was attacking the snake and he fell to the ground, along with Aurora who felt darkness envelope her.

35

Happiness

Pearl was shouting her name, but she had red eyes. Why did Pearl have red eyes? Aurora wondered, she had blue eyes. No, cats couldn't talk. Suddenly Pearl transformed into the snake and then he started to say her name more urgently.

No, Aurora realized, Pearl wasn't shouting her name nor was the snake. It was Ivy, she slowly opened her eyes and looked around.

"Oh thank goodness you are awake." Ivy sighed in relief

"Ivy! Are you okay? What about all the others? Pearl? The snake? And-"

"Oh god, enough. I am fine, the others are right here in the hospital, its night and we were all sleeping then you started to mutter something and I woke up" Ivy cut her off and explained

"Pearl is in the vet clinic and is being treated nicely. The other pets are found and returned to their owners. The snake is dead and the school had decided to tell the world about its past."

Aurora breathed a big sigh of relief, everything was well.

"The past? But why?" She asked

"No idea" Ivy said shrugging

"Hey! We all are awake too" Eleanor said crossly waking up

"I'm not" Leila said sleepily

"Now you are!" Violet laughed, bolting up and throwing a pillow at her

"Hey! Nobody gets away with throwing pillows at me!" Leila jokingly said back and threw a pillow at Violet

"Oh well, I am bored" Elsa said yawning and went to search the "patient use" cupboard.

"Ivy?"

"Yeah"

"The snake's body? What happened to it"

"I don't know Aurora, nor it matters"

Ivy was right, the snake's body defenetly did not matter. They had good friends, a safe school, a loving family, what else could they need?

"Yo! Guys, I found gummy bears and ludo in here," Elsa said, bringing the game box and the packet of treats.

Leila and Violet abandoned their pillow fight to eat a few.

"You wanna play? And I'm gonna take colour blue!" Aurora added quickly

"Nah, Violet and I already have our game" Leila said waving the offer away and took the pillows from the other's girl's bed too.

"Mine is green!" Ivy exclaimed

"Red" Eleanor said

"Yellow" Elsa said

"Your turn first aurora" Ivy said, handing the dice to her

Aurora took it from her, smiling. She was lucky, very lucky indeed to have these amazing friends by her side. She popped a jelly into her mouth, stretched and rolled the dice.

It landed at six.

36

Last Day

1 month later

A small ray of sunshine seeped through the blinds. Aurora got up sleepily, mainly because Pearl was AGAIN pawing at her face. She threw the duvet off her and looked at the blue dress with a jeans top, wondering what her best dress was doing there until she remembered! Today was the end of the first year and also the start of the summer holidays.

Aurora quickly took a bath and wore the dress with incarnate flower designs. The jeans top had beautiful buttons and beads. She put a bow on her shiny silver hair and wore her low heel shiny shoes.

Stuffing some more stuff in her suitcases Aurora dragged it out of her room, from where it would be collected by the staff to be put in her parent's car.

The others hadn't got ready yet, so there was no use of heading to the student lounge. Aurora and the others house heads had planned a big party. All houses and pets included except horses for whom they had made a nice party in the stables themselves.

Aurora gazed around the room, she wouldn't be back here for another two months. Would the room change? She wondered, or would it stay the same? Only time will tell though, only time would tell.

She remembered after being discharged from the hospital she had met her parents first.

"You were very brave, even if you might have been a bit foolhardy" her mom said, hugging her.

"Because of that, we will reduce your one week grounding into one day" Her dad told Aurora.

After that media had surrounded her and her friends but they had decided to not say a word about it, uninterested, the camera people went back.

She remembered the news on the tv, the anger from the world.

"Pet academy's board has told us about its bad past, what do you have to say about it?" an interviewer had asked a random person

"I say that pet academy had no right to keep us in the dark about its past while we trust it and send our children there. I do say the school is very good and I would not have seen its past. but if it had told us it wouldn't have been a shock" the women replied.

On an another vedio, where the news women had interviewed miss. Miss. Victoria

"what would you like to say to everyone who thinks you have betrayed them?"

"I would like to say that this school has changed from its previous version" And then Miss. Victoria got up, wore her coat and went away.

Someone knocked on the door, snapping Aurora out from her thoughts. She took her purse and Pearl and went out to meet her friends.

In the party hall of the student lounge, Aurora sat on a table, one leg over another with Valentina, Emily and Mia.

Ivy played table tennis in a distance with Lisa.

"How beautiful this year was" Valentina pondered, sipping her orange juice.

"It certainly was" Emily replied, stirring her cold coffee.

"What do you guys think about next year?" Mia asked, flinging her long beautiful hair behind her shoulders.

Aurora saw Ivy whoop; happy she had won. "Better or worse, but whatever it is, we will be ready for it"

<h1 style="text-align:center">Epilgou</h1>

1 month later

Aurora Stargaze stirred her hot chocolate, looking at the sky. It had beautiful wisps of orange and bluish clouds. The sky itself was a pinkish haze, it was about to be sunset.

Today the kitty crown was about to have a sleepover party. They hadn't met each other for about a month after the summer holidays started and Aurora smiled as she recalled her memories.

She had met all of her friends' parents, and then realized their parents had started to talk, knowing adults the girls decided to play some games.

In their last day togather in year first, they indulged in games of tag, hide and seek and ice water, laughing like idiots in the sun.

They had decided to meet in the holidays but weren't able to do so in the first month because Eleanor had gone to Paris for a vacation and Aurora had visited her grandparents.

After that, Aurora decided for a nice sleepover party at her house. She had spread fluffy sleeping mattresses on the floor, cute cushions and pillows. They would watch frozen two and Anabelle while eating lots of popcorn and drinking hot chocolate along with brownies. The others were bringing cookies, a cake, donuts, marshmallows and Ivy was bringing Californian sushi rolls as a reminder of their adventure.

Aurora was waiting for Ivy and the others until the doorbell rang, she ran from her balcony and opened the door. Ivy hugged her while ginger and Pearl ran off to the cat tree to play.

"Oh I've missed you so much" Ivy squealed

"me too, now let's go to my room" Aurora told.

They both chatted about stuff, as the others weren't coming yet Aurora put on the tv and gave Pearl and ginger some cat fish biscuits.

The doorbell rang again and Ivy ran to open the door, Eleanor, Elsa, Leila and Violet had came. They talked while Aurora took their small bags containing food and clothes and put them in the corner.

"The weather's so nice"

"Aww, look at the cats, they seemed to have missed each other"

"I enjoy home but school was great"

"are you in touch with the others?"

"Hey guys! I brought something for you all" Ivy shouted above the noise

Ivy handed small boxes to everyone, inculuding herself

"I love it how you brought one for yourself, even though you knew what was in it" Aurora noticed

"yeah, I didn't wanna ruin the surprise" Ivy admitted

"Hmm, it looks like a jewellery box" Eleanor pondered

Aurora looked inside and sucked her breath, inside was a beautiful silver coloured chain with a beautiful butterfly shaped locket, it was royal blue and had a lining of shining artificial diamonds inside.

Ivy's locket was green, Elsa's was sky blue while Eleanor's was a bright shade of yellow. Leila 's butterfly was pink and Violet's, surprisingly was a shiny black

"They are so beautiful, thank you Ivy" Aurora thanked

"Same, thanks" Leila agreed

"I love them" Elsa said

"You're welcome, I brought them with my pocket money. They were on sale on E-bay, also, they have speciel feature. If you press the butterfly hard enough, it will make noise if anyone wearing the necklace is near, cool right?" Ivy explained

"That is so cool, let's try it" Eleanor suggested.

Everybody pressed their locked and the room was filled with a musical beep.

"Let's not tell anyone about it, it would be like a secret kitty crown icon!" Aurora said.

Everyone agreed.

It was sunset and the girls were preparing to cut the cake. Aurora went out to the balcony, Pearl following her.

This is happiness She thought as she watched the clouds for exquisite orange and pink patterns.

A flock of parrots flew overhead, sqauwking and chirping. Pearl looked at them and snarled, Aurora laughed.

How much pet academy had changed her, and how much she had changed pet academy. Aurora had a feeling that the king anaconda wasn't the only hybrid they'd have to save the school from, but she was excited.

"Come on Aurora! Stop sunwatching and come eat cake!" Ivy called her from inside.

"Okay, Coming!" Aurora called back.

The sun was now a big orange ball that hung just above the horizen, ready to sink down. Around it the clouds had orangish hues, when the sun set, Aurora went inside. Pearl went with her with a last glance at the sky, or perhaps the birds.

Next year they will have adventures, perhaps bettter then the ones they got this year. But whatever it was, they were ready.

Hello Readers!

When I first sat down to write pet academy, it was just suposed to be a short story on my blog (ExplorerSidra.com.blogspot). But then I found out that Aurora's story couldn't be finished in such a short space. She needed a book.

So I wrote Pet academy. In between, I almost gave up on the book, but then my mom made me understand that the book needs to be comepleted.

I had thought the story was useless, but then I read it again and wrote and weaved it into the book you are reading today.

I would like to point out that the pet care points in this book and the pet breeds are all real, but the king anaconda and the pet academy, along with the forest are purely fictional. Any mistakes you find are purely mine and I apologize in adavance.

Pets are an important part in our lives, and some of you have probably experienced that wonderful feeling of having an Animal friend.

When I was younger, I remember sitting under or on trees. Looking at the squirrels and hearing birds. Birdwatching, as also mentioned in the book is an amazing activity, you just need to look at the birds and write about them.

In this book, Pearl is very well mannered and so are most of the pets that are mentioned. The bonds that our main charachters shares can be acheived in real life, and so can be the well mannered animals. Sometimes you have to pamper them and sometimes be a little strict with them, like when they start eating your rug.

I would like to say, as a disclaimer that going into a wild forest unprotected is not a very good idea. Any other dangerous things done in this book, like climbing of a ladder and going into a rotting building is not reccomended.

If you want to read more of my books, I reccomend "When The Wolves Howl" It was my first ever book.

I hope you enjoyed this book as much I loved writing it
A cat's cuddle,
Sidra Khan
P.S. The Story has not ended

Acknowledgements

First of all, as should be I will thank my god, Allah, its because of him I was able to write this book and weave the story of Pet Academy.

I would like to give thanks to my mom as unless she hadn't encouraged me to continue this book, you would not be reading this.

A big shout out to my dad who was probably eager then me to see this story have a happy ending. And its because of him I am able to publish this book.

A note of appreciation to Miss. Nida for tips on english grammer and its because of her that I am able to put Aurora's story in words.

Thanks to the notion press team for spending their time in my book and believing in me.

And most of all, thanks to whoever's reading this because this book wouldn't be possible without you, dear reader.

We'll Meet Again,
Sidra Khan